TROUBLE AT EVERY TURN

A SLIM CALHOUN, BULL MORRISON
WESTERN

JOHNNY GUNN

WOLFPACK
PUBLISHING
— EST 2013 —

WOLFPACK
PUBLISHING
— EST 2013 —

Trouble At Every Turn
A Slim Calhoun, Bull Morrison Western

Paperback Edition
© Copyright 2020 Johnny Gunn

Wolfpack Publishing
6032 Wheat Penny Avenue
Las Vegas, NV 89122

wolfpackpublishing.com

Paperback ISBN 978-1-64734-031-5
eBook ISBN 978-1-64734-032-2

TROUBLE AT EVERY TURN

CHAPTER 1

"You gonna let one little bullet ruin your day?" U.S. Marshal Bull Morrison swaggered into Virginia City's hospital to see his deputy, Slim Calhoun.

"It wasn't one little bullet; it was four little bullets called buck shot. Embarrassing."

"Shoulda laid out flat on the ground. Rump was sticking out from that rock you were huggin'."

"You here to make me feel better or get me all angry and upset? Doc says if I can get my pants on, I can leave this miserable place."

Slim Calhoun had chased three men deep into Six-Mile Canyon, trapped them at the Butter's Mill, and got in a fierce firefight. Two of the three were mortally wounded, but the third almost managed to escape when he shot Calhoun. Calhoun said in his report, "I was so angry I jumped up and shot that ugly old fool four times and then once more just to be sure."

"I'm here to roust you out, Slim. Major wants us back in San Francisco pronto like. I've booked us on the evening express to Reno where we'll change trains to the city." Morrison turned to leave then turned back. "Might want to bring a cushion for that long ride on wooden benches." He was laughing hard as he scuttled out the door.

"Funny man," Calhoun said. He threw the empty bedpan and enjoyed watching it bounce off his boss. "Shoulda ducked," he yelled.

Bull Morrison was just that, a bull of a man. He stood about five feet nine inches tall, weighed in at one ninety-five and carried no fat. There was a brutal and ugly scar that ran across his face, from high on his left temple to his right jaw. The scar brightened with the level of his anger or desire to fight. According to Calhoun, the man combed his hair with his fingers and a wash rag once or twice a week.

He joined the Marshal Service during the War Between the States, served two years in The Territories and had been in the western division since. His great joy in life was fighting, his second, drinking, and if he could combine the two, he called it a fine day, indeed. He mounted his horse, still chuckling some, and rode up the steep hills of the Comstock to the Virginia and Truckee train station.

Winter was settling in with a vengeance, the wind howling down off Sun Mountain with curtains of heavy snow riding the waves. Bull Morrison looked at the weather the same as he looked at life. That is, you can't change the weather, live with it. If you work your way into a situation you can't change, live with it.

"Best damn deputy a marshal could ask for," he mumbled. "I love to give him hell. Wish I knew what the major wants. All he said was to get there fastest. Why do these things always happen in the winter?" Morrison was wearing a bearskin coat and by the time he reached the train station it probably weighed in at sixty pounds or more.

IT WOULD NOT HAVE BEEN fun to watch as Slim Calhoun fought to get his pants on. The pain from the four deep puncture wounds in his rump hurt like hell and the bandages caught on everything. He was red in the face and sweating when he fastened the top button on his pants, and there was a definite limp as he made his way out of the hospital. By the time he reached the train station, he was sure all four wounds were bleeding again.

Slim Calhoun came from Missouri farm country, stood about six feet tall and carried about a hundred and eighty pounds on his strong frame. His longish light-colored hair and sly grin tend to make the ladies want to get close. He rarely said no. Slim had a wicked sense of humor, often aimed at Morrison, but also in general. He saw humor in some awkward situations sometimes.

"Major give you any idea of what he wants? We surely busted up that Sinclair bunch. They hit five banks before we stopped 'em. I was lookin' forward to a week or so in this exciting city. I've never heard this much noise ever. Bells, whistles, steam engines at every mine, my God, it's bedlam"

"Got a second wire from him," Morrison said. They got their horses loaded on the train and found their seats. They'd take this train down to Carson City, then another north to Reno, before catching a Western Pacific to Sacramento. From there, it was a paddlewheel steamer to San Francisco. "Something about a conspiracy to blow up federal buildings in California, Nevada, and Colorado. I'll let you read it when we get moving. Did you bring a bottle?"

Calhoun was laughing when he reached into his bundle for a bottle and tin cups. "It's a rule of the road, isn't it?"

"It's a Morrison rule of the road." He poured, took a drink, and handed the telegram to Calhoun. "You might remember one of those names. Colonel Jupiter? Didn't we meet him in Texas, right after the war? A corporal in the Rebs army, a deserter who turned outlaw and gave himself a new name and rank."

"I remember him. Corporal Patrick Mullins, deserter, killer, rapist, and ugly as sin. He's been successful as a bank robber according to the latest sheets on him. He should have a scar across his forehead from the front sight on my Winchester. I whopped that boy hard and the damn sheriff let him escape."

Calhoun took the wire and read it twice before handing it back. "Looks like we might have a bit of work to do." He had a delightful little boy's grin as he took a long drink from his tin cup and tried to get comfortable as the train chugged its way off the Comstock. "Yup, should have ducked."

Making the change in Carson City would have been an easy one except that one of those winter storms that blast along the eastern flanks of the Sierra Nevada decided that night was prime time for another hit. Winds of near hurricane force drove snow horizontally. Moving their horses from one car to another became a circus event for the marshals, and by the time they were on the thirty mile ride to Reno, Bull Morrison was ready to kill anyone or anything, Slim Calhoun was bleeding and wanted to drink the flask dry.

"The rest of this trip had best be an easy one," Morrison said. "Here's something for you to contemplate, Slim. Why would a confederate deserter want to blow up federal buildings in the far west? Washington? I might give that some thought. But San Francisco? Denver?"

"Why and how an outlaw's mind works is nothing I plan to contemplate, Bull. It's bad enough when we bring them in alive that we have to be near them." He reached for his tin cup and bottle.

CHAPTER 2

SAN FRANCISCO'S WATERFRONT WAS KNOWN AS ONE OF THE ROUGHEST areas west of the Rocky Mountains, and in second place would be the deep-water port of Stockton, California. The town where the San Joaquin River became part of the San Francisco Bay, along with the Sacramento River, bustled with commerce, intrigue, and lawlessness. Three men were meeting in a sailor's saloon along a busy dock.

"To make this work, we need a diversion," a man called Major John T. Ivory said. Ivory was a wiry little man with dark eyes, deeply bronzed skin from hours in the sun, and long black hair that he kept in a braid that almost reached his waist. "I'm more in favor of hitting them on the road, not the main buildings. Robbing a train or stage is easier than a bank, remember."

"We're not robbing a bank, Ivory, we're blowing up the very building where they make the damn money. The mint." Colonel Jupiter stood up and paced around the table. "I want as much of their gold as we can carry, but more than that, Ivory. I want those buildings destroyed, eliminated."

Jupiter had never been a good soldier, he never served above the rank of corporal and had deserted at the first opportunity, yet he had this strange hatred of all things Union. His family was dirt poor, didn't own slaves, hell, didn't own anything. They held no real ties to Virginia, the Confederacy, or hatred of the Union. Jupiter was hiding from a patrol sent out to arrest him when he heard that the war was over.

Instead of jubilation, he became an angry man, an outlaw in the name of the Confederacy. He robbed banks in its name, robbed trains in its name, and now, it seemed, planned to rob and destroy the nation's western mints in its name.

"You're a fool Jupiter," Ivory said, "but I'll ride with you for the money. There is no Confederacy, never will be one, but there is gold and silver in those buildings. That's all I want." Unlike Jupiter, Ivory had been a good soldier, rising to the rank of sergeant and served in Pennsylvania, Virginia, and Louisiana. His specialty had been blowing up railroads, bridges, and tunnels.

The third man called himself Major Orville Conroy. He had served as a private in a supply company and never saw any combat, stole and sold most of what was supposed to be distributed to the troops. He, too, was in this gang for the money. Only Jupiter had other motivations.

"I say we start with the new mint in Carson City, then blow up the San Francisco Mint, leaving Denver for last," Jupiter said. "Linda Bricky is in Carson City now. She will supply us with all the plans for the building."

Bricky had been Jupiter's sidekick for several years and was known as one of the best at planning bank robberies. She and Jupiter had known each other before the war and when he deserted, he looked her up. They had paper out from Virginia to California.

Bricky dressed elegantly and used her beauty and charm to learn all the necessary things about a bank, a banker's schedule, and when and where the money would be. She wanted to make one big splash, one heist that would bring her furs, silks, and feathers, rooms at the finest hotels, and entrance to even larger banks. She also was looking for a more refined partner.

Ivory listened as Jupiter spent the next half hour detailing how important it would be to fully destroy the new mint, how it would erode confidence in the Union, and bring them glory. Ivory's thoughts continued to zero in on the money. Gold. Silver. To hell with blowing up the building when you can take the gold and silver when they ship it. Time to make my own plans, build my own operation.

"We should leave at once and get ourselves established. Linda has already rented a cabin for us on the west side of town. She's working with the man who is in charge of building. Some big shot in the town. She can get at least one of us a construction job."

"That would be me," Conroy said. "I've done a lot of that kind of work before the war. They're building with stone I think makes it harder to blow it up."

"Not really," Ivory said. "If you can blow up a train, you can sure as hell blow up a stone building." He was shaking his head, wondering if either one of these dolts had thought what the dynamite would do to the gold and silver coins. His mind was made up to form his own group and attack the shipments, not the building. How to do that without letting either Jupiter or Conroy know would be his test.

Once we get our hands on the plans for the building, I'll make sure we also get our hands on when the shipments will be made. Then, adios to Jupiter, maybe for good.

"I'M GONNA NEED TO see a doc as soon as we get to Sacramento,

Bull. I've ripped those wounds wide open and I'm sure they're infected." Slim Calhoun had tried his best to change the dressing in the tiny railcar washroom several times on the long ride over the Sierra Nevada, and the pain had increased each time.

"I'm ridin' with a crybaby," Morrison chuckled. "It's bad enough that the trip is gonna take at least three more days because of this blasted storm, but I gotta share my space with a cry-baby." He had to quickly duck the right cross that threatened his jaw, and then laughed right out, seeing Calhoun cringe from his own pain. "There should be a doc on the steamboat, Slim. If not, I'll go on and you catch up."

"That'll work. I won't be any good to you until it's fixed up right. Needed one night at that hospital. The vagaries of war, eh?"

Morrison just looked at him. "What the hell's a vagary?"

Calhoun had to laugh, found the bottle and tin cups, and emptied the bottle. "If anyone asks how far it is from Virginia City to Sacramento, tell them it's one bottle far." They chuckled and could feel the train begin to slow some. "This idea of blowing up the mint buildings doesn't make a lot of sense, Bull. Got any ideas rolling around in that thick skull?"

"Yes, I do, Deputy," Morrison snarled, then chuckled. "I think it's damn stupid, but on the other hand, if the idea of someone blowing up the mints would keep people like us busy, they could simply be planning a robbery."

"Diversion," Calhoun said. "We're working to solve the conspiracy and they're planning a robbery. So, Mr. Marshal, sir, we work on solving the robbery while pretending to stop the conspiracy."

"Yup." Morrison drained his tin cup as the train pulled to a screeching stop near the waterfront in California's capitol city. The Sacramento River was running full and a steamer was standing by for the run to San Francisco. There was a doctor on board, so the marshals got their horses and gear on board well before shoving off time.

"Bet you won't be flirtin' with that girl again," Doctor Montgomery snickered. "Fathers and shotguns do a fine job protecting their little darlings."

Bull Morrison laughed right out. "Give him hell, Doc." He had to leave the little office and find the first officer of the boat. "Major said if anything new came up he'd leave word with him. I'll see you back in the cabin, lover-boy."

The wound cleaned up nicely, the trip down river, through the delta, and into San Francisco Bay was uneventful, and the marshals arrived at the federal building later the next day. "Didn't find out until late yesterday, boys, but it seems that this Patrick Mullins/Colonel Jupiter fool has returned to Carson City. You didn't have to leave, after all."

Major Silas Lambert was Chief Marshal, Western Division, a veteran of the War Between the States, the Mexican War, and now, many years in the marshal service. "Your butt healed up, Calhoun? Good job on that Sinclair gang. I've got you two re-booked back to Nevada, leaving tomorrow morning."

Lambert was known for never speaking in full sentences, always running thoughts together, and rarely smiling. "Get a good night's sleep, stay out of trouble, and let me know when you get there." He waved the two off with a flick of his hand, and they were chuckling all the way out of the building.

"Sure glad we got here in a rush." Morrison pointed down the steep hill. "There's a saloon near the docks that usually has a pot of chili on the fire. Should be our first stop, eh?"

The bitter cold of Nevada was replaced with the damp, foggy cold of San Francisco Bay, and it seemed to energize Morrison. He walked down the steep hill as if he were about to meet the most charming and attractive princess in Europe. "I assume you're almost running because the chili is so good. Wouldn't have anything to do with the pleasure of their grog, would it?"

"It's the fog, Slim. The fog in San Francisco has a flavor all its own. You southern boys just don't understand the poetry of the weather, do you?"

"Poetry of the weather? That's a new one, Bull Morrison. I understand the music of a good bourbon, the scent of fine gin, but the poetry of the weather? I think I'll just forget you even said such a thing."

Morrison was humming something as they descended into the rowdy dock area for their one night in the City by the Bay.

CHAPTER 3

"BULL MORRISON," THE BARMAN YELLED OUT WHEN THE TWO WALKED into Johnny's Little Texas. "Back in town, eh? Well, remember the house rules. Don't be picking fights, no gun play, and be nice to the ladies."

"I don't play with guns, Dirk. There ain't no play with a gun. They're for serious business only. The ladies are safe from me, maybe not Slim, and I don't pick fights, they pick me. Bring us a gallon of chili and a couple of bottles, please."

Calhoun had his arm around one of the serving girls and she was doing what she could to get as close to the long, tall, deputy marshal as she could. "You good at bringing chili with those bottles?" He asked. She bumped him gently with her hips, smiled, and danced off toward the kitchen. "Nice girl," he said, slipping into a chair at a table near the fireplace.

"Hope the major has a packet for us tomorrow morning," Morrison said. He was trying to ignore Calhoun and poured the drinks. He started to take a drink and was bumped hard from behind, spilling half his glass.

"What the hell?" Morrison howled, jumping to his feet.

"Scoot your damn chair in, mate, so a man can get through," a man dressed as a seaman said. He was five-seven at best, and less than one-fifty. His arms were bare and covered in tattoos. "No thought for anyone but yourself, eh mate?"

Morrison roared, swung a mighty right and knocked the sailor ten feet back, knocking over a table on the way. Morrison stood in surprise when the sailor jumped to his feet, leaped forward, and drove a boot into Morrison's face, knocking him to the ground. The sailor jumped on the big marshal and tried to get a choke hold on his thick neck.

Morrison knocked the little man's hands away, drove a fist up three times into his face, flung him back and got to his feet in time to take another kick to the face. This time, though, he caught the foot, twisted all the way around, hearing the leg break at the knee. He let go and let the man fall to the grimy floor.

"Everything me mother told me about life tells me I should kick your head in, mate," Morrison shouted. "But she raised a gentleman, so I won't." He turned back to the table, said, "Ah, to hell with it," and drove his boot deep into the man's stomach." He sat back down, retrieved his glass and drained what was left in it.

"I didn't start it, Dirk," he shouted out to the barman. He was laughing as he re-filled his glass and Calhoun yelled out a warning. The sailor was crawling across the floor and about to throw a dagger into Morrison's back. Two shots rang out, one from Calhoun, one from Morrison, and the sailor died.

Dirk walked over, shaking his head. "You had to come in here, didn't you, Bull. Drink your drinks, eat your chili, and go home, Bull Morrison. You're bad for business."

"Didn't start it," was all Bull said. Calhoun had to chuckle, watching the two men shake their heads at each other. "Didn't."

"I COULD HAVE EATEN TWO MORE BOWLS OF THAT CHILI," Calhoun said. The two were in the stables getting saddled up for the short ride to the docks. "Marybelle was too anxious for us to get to her place. How did the rest of your night go? Or, maybe I shouldn't ask."

"I'm here," is all Bull Morrison said. His face had bruises, he had a fat lip, and Slim noticed his knuckles were skinned and bruised as well. Morrison pulled the cinch tight and reached into a saddlebag. "Major sent these for us. Background on three men, Jupiter included. How's your butt?"

"You're starting to sound like the major," Calhoun said. "Marybelle was a fair nurse, too," he chuckled. "You and Dirk get things figured out? He wasn't really upset, was he?"

"After two of those fellers in the back told him that I didn't start it, that the fool came at me with a knife, he calmed down. Seems that little jerk was a troublemaker and been asked to leave more than once. Got any thoughts on this bombing stuff?"

"Still think it's to keep us busy while a robbery of some kind takes place. Does the major want us to work with anyone in Carson City? Local city marshal? County sheriff?"

"Never mentioned it. We'll work it out when we get there. I'm gonna sleep on the boat, and drink on the train." He was making an attempt at a smile as they rode out of the barn and down the long hill to the docks.

"Is THIS THE BEST YOU COULD DO?" Colonel Jupiter was standing in front of a small cabin set in a grove of pine trees, just off a dirt road. "It's a mile into town. Damn."

Damn little peacock wouldn't be happy no matter what I found. He'd complain if he had to walk half a block. Linda Bricky was twenty-five, with light brown hair and dark brown eyes. She stood about five-five and weighed in at one twenty, soaking wet. Her mother was a beautiful Creole woman who had a dalliance with a Norwegian sailor in the warmth of a

New Orleans balmy night. Linda's temper equaled her beauty.

"You said you wanted a small cabin out of town, Patrick. That's what I gotcha. Don't like it? Too bad for you."

He bristled at being called Patrick: he had demanded that people call him Colonel or Jupiter. "You're pushing, girl. The others will be here shortly, and you can tell us what we need to know about this new mint. I can already smell the explosion."

"I can smell the money," she said. She walked into the cabin and through the main room into the kitchen. "I've got the papers on the table, here." The papers were the construction designs for the large building and Ivory would use them in order to know where to plant the explosives. He always emphasized that he wanted to destroy the building but not the gold and silver.

"Things like this have to be done with finesse," Ivory would say. "It's important that we destroy this building and it's equally important that we carry off the gold and silver."

"These design papers are what we'll need to pull this off right," Jupiter said. He shuffled through the papers as if he knew what he was looking at. Ivory would know: the little ex-corporal had no idea. "These will be just fine."

Linda snorted and pulled the pot of coffee from the hot stove. He really does think he's some sort of big shot. Colonel. He ain't no more a colonel than I'm a lady. She had to snort again with those thoughts. "I've got Conroy set to work on the construction gang. Abe Curry is the boss. Tell Conroy he doesn't want to give that old bastard a hard time." Linda Bricky laughed as she poured some whiskey in a cup and filled it with coffee. "People here in town call Curry the father of Carson City. He's got himself a temper."

"Well, what he won't have is a mint building when I get through with him," Jupiter said. "I'd like to have at least one more person on this job, somebody who could act as a lookout if needed, or as a decoy to draw guards away. Do you know anyone we could trust?"

"I'll think on it," Linda said. "Looks like Conroy and Ivory are here. I've got to get back to work. Tell Conroy to come to the work site when he gets settled." She said hello to Conroy and Ivory as they came into the kitchen.

"Ivory, will you walk me back to town? I want to tell you about how they're setting up all the vaults." He nodded and they slipped out of the cabin for the walk back to town.

"You worried about something?" Ivory asked.

"I wouldn't call it worried so much as concerned. Of the three of you, why aren't you the leader? You were a combat sergeant in the war, they were deserters, you led men, they ran. I think this entire operation is a wheel with a missing cog."

John Ivory laughed, slipped his arm around her shoulder and squeezed with strong firm fingers. "Mullins calls himself Colonel Jupiter and I let him. He wants to call me major, and I let him. His whole scheme is to blow up the buildings to get even with the Union or some damn thing. I'm glad you feel the way you do. Let's get to know each other a little better and I'll tell you what my plans are."

"I have some, too," she murmured. She liked the feel of his arm around her shoulders, wanted it, actually. Saw the slight smile with the question in his eyes, and liked that, too. "I have a place near the railroad yards. We can be alone and talk some," she said. Her eyes said yes to his.

"TOWN'S GROWN SOME SINCE THE LAST TIME WE WERE HERE," Calhoun said, drawing a guffaw from Morrison. "Major has us set up in the St. Charles Hotel, across from the capitol building. I think you might be right not telling people who we are until we get a better idea of what we're up against."

"If anyone asks, we're cattle buyers or something like that," Bull said. "I'm gonna send a wire to Major Lambert and ask that he send another deputy. I asked for Squash Monroe. Hope he's available."

They got settled at the hotel and walked north to look at what was being built. "Those are big rocks," Morrison said. "The San Francisco Mint is substantial; this one might outdo it."

"Feller at the hotel said the stones are quarried just east of town here. Mighty fancy work those boys are doing." Slim Calhoun stepped right up to where the men were working.

"Recognize that feller over there?" Calhoun nodded toward a thin man trying to carry some heavy wood across the construction yard. "Looks like who the major described as Orville Conroy, doesn't he? That long stringy blond hair, the one leg not quite straight from a bullet wound? Sure looks like him to me."

"I think you're right. I wonder how the shifts work? We might want to see where he goes after work. Best way to find out anything is head for a near-by saloon, eh Calhoun?"

"Sounds reasonable to me. Even if we don't find answers, we win." He laughed and pointed. "There's one called The Palace Club across the street. Bet that's a busy place after shift."

They made their way across the bustling North Carson Street and into The Palace Club, a small, slightly dingy saloon with a long bar along the north wall. There were gaming tables and drinking tables scattered along the south wall, and four men standing at the far end of the bar when the two walked in.

Slim and Bull stood at the bar instead of taking a table, hoping they might learn a few things about shifts and people working on the new mint building. "A couple of beers, barman," Slim said, dropping a half-eagle on the bar. "Got anything to eat back there?"

"Don't serve food. It's a beer and whiskey bar, gentlemen. Might find some food at the Silver Queen down the street."

"Only if you want to die of food poisoning," one of the men at the end of bar laughed out. "Whiskey won't kill you, but their food might."

"Glad to know that," Morrison laughed. "Looks like a busy project across the street. We just got in town, what are they building over there?"

"That's the new United States Mint," the man said. "Mines up on the Comstock are so rich the government's building a mint right here. Worked there at the start."

"Not working now?" Bull asked.

"One of them big rocks fell off a wagon and crushed me leg. Won't never work again," he said. "Names Honeycutt. Just in town, eh? What's your line?"

"Cattle, mostly," Bull said. "I'm Morrison, this is my partner, Slim Calhoun. They make it right for you, with your ruined leg and all?"

"Said they will. Haven't yet. Abe Curry's a good man. He'll help me if the government doesn't."

"Those shifts over there work late? Day's getting on," Bull said.

"They'll be breakin' up in the next hour or so. The boss lady'll come prancing in here shortly and that will be the sign," he chuckled. "She don't show up until there's money flowing across the boards."

"Sounds like my kind of woman," Calhoun chuckled. "Better get us a couple more beers, there, barman. What's this lady's name?"

"Name's Irene," the barman said. "Irene Thorndyke. Came here from St. Louis, she says. Don't listen to those old geezers. She's a nice lady, easy to work for, and runs a clean table when she's dealing. She don't much cater to young pups puttin' on airs.

CHAPTER 4

IRENE THORNDYKE WAS NEARING FORTY BUT LOOKED FAR YOUNGER. Her reddish hair hung in long curls and waves, her green eyes sparkled, and she had a genuine laugh and smile for her customers. Irene had married an influential trader in western goods, furs, Indian beadwork, and baskets, and became flush with his early death. Saloons and gambling had always been an attraction, and money flowed in western mining towns.

When Irene read about the Comstock and its incredible wealth, near Carson City, the state's capitol, and the building of a mint, she took the first train west. The Palace Club was a grubby little saloon almost in the center of town. The train station was close, the new Capitol Building, almost built, was close, and the new mint was going up across the street. She paid cash for the place and had no intentions of sprucing it up. She told her friends it had personality. What it had, was steady customers.

"Hello, Leroy. What a nice day," she said. She walked the length of the saloon and slipped behind the bar, giving everyone a big smile. She was wearing an emerald dress that emphasized her generous bosom, tiny waist, and swaying hips. "Mr. Honeycutt," she said, "How's that leg of yours?"

"About half-full of whiskey," he laughed. "Must be quittin' time across the street."

"Oh, my," she laughed. "I guess it is." It wasn't five minutes and the saloon was filled with men spending money, laughing, and joshing each other. Irene moved up and down the bar, filling glasses, pouring beer, and flirting with many.

"I think I like this lady," Slim Calhoun said. "She knows how to work the crowd."

"I bet she knows a lot more than that," Bull Morrison said. "I think you need to get to know her. See if she can work for us without knowing that she is. I'm gonna work on this Honeycutt feller." Morrison moved down to the end of the bar, next to the injured worker.

"Buy you a beer? Need to pick your brains about this town. Ain't been here before," Morrison said. "Guess we won't eat at that joint you were talking about. Where can a cattle buyer find a good steak?"

That's all it took, and Honeycutt and Morrison were in deep conversation about cattle, how to raise them, how to butcher them, and how to cook them the best. Slim Calhoun watched as Morrison led Honeycutt into slowly talking about people associated with the town's leadership, the building of the mint, and some of the people involved in the building.

"Don't think I've seen you, before," Irene said. She was standing across the bar from Calhoun giving the tall deputy marshal a long look. "Thirsty?"

He almost said, And hungry, but didn't. His eyes on the other hand spent some time enjoying the lady. "A cold beer would be fine. Name's Calhoun, Slim Calhoun. Just got in town."

"You came to the right place, Mr. Calhoun. We have the coldest beer in Carson City."

"And other attractions, I see," he said. A sly grin, a nod of the head, and she responded with the slightest tinkle of a laugh.

"A man of few words and many ideas, I do believe," she answered. There was an equally sly grin and just the slightest nod of her head. "Are you a part of the mint project over there?"

"No, I'm in the cattle business, but that is quite an undertaking." He took the time to look up and down the bar and around at the tables. The place was full of men drinking off their day's hard work. Lamps were gritty but lit, the floors had been swamped, spittoons emptied, beer barrels rolled into place. The Palace Club was a beer and whiskey saloon, ideal for the working man.

"I assume you're in favor of the mint project. Where can a hungry man find a good steak in this town? We asked before and Mr. Honeycutt down there told us about a place sure to poison us. That's my partner talking to him now."

"Honeycutt's full of answers," she laughed. "The best steak is at Ace's House. It's a small saloon and gambling hall for those that dress in fine linen and hotel for those that travel in style. Ace Hardy runs the place, dressed in wool pants, silk vests, and string ties."

"And where would a man with dusty boots and canvas trousers eat?" Slim Calhoun asked. "I'm not the silk vest type."

Before she could answer a ruckus broke out at the end of the bar. "You try to shove me aside one more time and I'm gonna rip your face off," Bull Morrison shouted into a hefty stone cutter's dirty face. "Find your own damn space."

The stone cutter had shoulders like a bull moose, fists like a gorilla's, and the foul breath of a man who lived on whiskey and beer. "I drink right here," he snarled. He grabbed Morrison's coat and tried to move him aside. His two hundred pounds and massive muscles sent Morrison five feet back where he fell onto a table filled with beer mugs.

"Damn my soul," Morrison howled. He was on his feet and

with two quick steps smashed into the big worker. He drew blood from the filthy man's nose with one punch and found himself back on the table with a seriously cut upper lip. The stone cutter followed Morrison onto the table, which collapsed under the combined weight. The two huge men wrestled through two more tables, hammering each other with blows that would stop the average man.

It was less than one minute into the fight and two shots from a forty-five went through the roof and brought it to an end. "Both of you, on your feet," Irene Thorndyke said, waving the heavy revolver back and forth at them. "You," she said, pointing at Morrison. "You drink over there. You, Endicott, you drink over there." She pointed at the other end of the bar. "Endicott, you pay for one of those tables. You, Mr. Calhoun's partner, you pay for the other. Now, drink and be happy, gentlemen."

She walked back behind the bar, that wonderful smile back, and slipped the revolver back in its nest under the bar. "Leroy, can you watch the bar for a while? Mr. Calhoun and I are going out for supper. We'll be back a little later."

Morrison picked himself up off the floor, gave Calhoun a crooked, blood encrusted smile, and stepped back up to the bar. "Mr. Honeycutt, you should have warned me that I was about to meet a freight train. That man packs a damn fine punch."

"How long have you lived here, Linda?" John Ivory and Linda Bricky were sitting at a table in the small kitchen of her cabin. "I've heard Jupiter talk about you, but I didn't have any idea you were so young. He's a fool if he don't slap a brand on you."

"That won't never happen, John T." She laughed. "Patrick won't never own me. What do you mean he talks about me?" She bristled at the thought and got up quickly. "Don't need to hear something like that." She was pacing around the kitchen wondering just what it might be that Jupiter would talk about. "If he was to talk about anything it would be how many times I saved his butt."

"I just had the impression that," and he paused, looked around the room, trying to say the right words. "Maybe, you two were together. I hope I was wrong. Jupiter ain't right for any woman."

She had to laugh. "He sure ain't. And for sure he ain't right for me. No, John T., we ain't together in any way. He knew my brother during the war and helped him desert, run away. My brother was killed during a bank robbery somewhere in Kansas and Patrick brought me the news."

"The only reason I'm in on this operation," Ivory said, "is for the gold. I don't give a damn about blowin' up the buildings, but it will help in getting close to the gold. Personally, I think Jupiter is off his rocker. Steal the gold in transit, is my plan." He laughed and drank some coffee. "How about you?"

"He can't think past his anger," she said. "What's worse, he doesn't have anything but his stupid self to be angry about. The confederacy don't mean nothing to him, before the war he had never heard the word union." The two of them laughed at that and Linda came to the table to stand near Ivory.

"He doesn't have any idea how to plan or get information. I helped him plan a couple of bank jobs, got information on trains for him, and he brought me out here for this job. I'm with you, John T. It's the money, the gold, that counts, and I'm gettin' my full share this time. Bastard held out on me and I'm gettin' what's mine this time."

She glanced quickly at him, found him looking at her. He's a hungry man, not that big or strong. He knows what he wants, I might be part of that, and I'm ready. "I tried to tell

Patrick his ideas were goofy. We should wait until the mint is operating and hijack the gold and silver coins when they're being shipped. This whole operation is stupid."

John T. Ivory tightened up visibly and Linda Bricky wondered if maybe she had gone too far. Ivory smiled and motioned her over toward him. "I think maybe the two of us can work a little closer on this, Linda. It's the gold and silver that's most important. Besides, lovely lady, we both know what we really want, don't we?" His eyes were devouring the girl and she was fascinated by the ornery veteran, so much different from Jupiter.

Wiry little bastard with long braided hair is scary dangerous, but I wonder what would happen if he faced real danger. Men never are what they think they are. She stepped back and let her gaze settle on him.

She hadn't seen a man with hair that reached his waist, braided. He wasn't a big man, this John T. Ivory, she thought, but carried himself as if he was. He was offering a partnership, she thought, and it was more than robbing mints or chasing coaches. It was a way of life.

"I'd like that very much, John T." She walked around the table and slipped onto his lap. "It is gold we're talking about, isn't it?"

She heard a murmured yes as their lips closed on each other. Gold and silver have fascinating ways of bringing people together.

"ABOUT TIME YOU GOT DOWN HERE. Have a good night, did you?" Bull Morrison was on his second cup of coffee in the hotel café, waiting for Calhoun. Slim took a double take, held in a chuckle, seeing a fat, sliced lip, a blackened eye, and a couple of lumps on the forehead.

"I did indeed," he said, not trying to hide the smile. "Looks like you had a splendid night as well. You and Mr. Endicott continued your dance, did you?" Calhoun got a nasty look back from Morrison and had to laugh. "I even learned a few things, some of which have to do with our current assignment." He sat down as the waitress a buxom young Mexican woman came to the table. "Have you ordered?" He asked Bull who shook his head.

"I'll have a steak and half a dozen eggs all mixed up," Slim Calhoun said.

"Make mine two steaks and half a dozen eggs," Bull Morrison said. He turned to Slim. "Regarding our assignment, what did you learn?"

"There's a lot of politics of course in the siting and building of the mint, but in general the population is fully in favor. I think we might be better off letting people know who we are, maybe not why we're here, but who we are. I picked up a few names of local leaders who might be able to help us."

"Any background noise on disruption of building the mint? Like blowing it up? The problem with being in a mining environment when investigating the possibility of blowing up buildings is the availability of explosives. Everyone has some. Everyone's a prospector," Bull laughed. "Dynamite, fuse cord, blasting caps everywhere."

"Makes me remember when we chased those fugitives around Angel's Camp and that one fool blew up half the town. Got all excited about something and fired his rifle into the hardware store. Old man Swenson had fifteen hundred pounds of dynamite stored in there."

They were laughing, remembering how three buildings all but vanished in a giant orange bloom. Conversations continued through their breakfast and out onto the main street. "What are your plans for today, Bull?"

"I think you're right about letting people know the marshal service is in town. This Henry Honeycutt is quite the character. He seems to know everyone, and he has offered to take me about to see the whole operation, even to meet the man responsible for getting the mint here. Man's name is Abe Curry and he seems to be the one who first established the town itself."

"Irene mentioned him several times last night. There are federal building inspectors here that we should stay as far away from as possible," he chuckled. Morrison laughed right out. "The people who will be actually running the mint have their own security people, too."

"We'll stay away from them as well," Bull Morrison laughed. "We're here for criminal investigation only, not security. If the marshal service knows about this threat, I'm sure the treasury people do."

"I'm supposed to meet with a young lady who knows our man Orville Conroy from the project," Calhoun said. "Let's meet for beer at The Palace Club a little later."

"Good. Squash Monroe is due in today or tomorrow. Get some serious investigating done. Not all this other stuff. I'm going to try and get Squash hired on, undercover of course, at the building. Try to get him assigned to wherever Conroy is working."

"Your investigation going to include tearing up saloons and things?" Slim Calhoun snickered. He had to duck a long, arcing, right fist, laughing as he danced away. "See you shortly."

CHAPTER 5

"Where have you been, Ivory? Damn it, we need to stay together or sure as hell someone will know what we're doing." Jupiter was angry at everyone, lately, was yelling at Orville Conroy when he didn't come straight to the cabin after work, hounding Linda Bricky hourly, and now jumping down Ivory's throat.

"My job is to blow up the mint, Jupiter," Ivory snapped back. "I just stored a couple of hundred pounds of dynamite in our shed back there. Get off my back. You might call yourself a colonel talking to others, you ain't my damn boss. We're all in this together. What's Conroy know about the timetable? I still need to pick up a reel of fuse cord."

"I don't like you being gone for days at a time, John, that's all." Jupiter's demeanor changed quickly. Was it because he knew he needed John T. Ivory and his knowledge of blasting? Or was it that John T. Ivory scared the hell out of him. He proved his cowardice running like a crying baby from the battlefield; was he unable to stand up to this real soldier?

"I went to Virginia City and bought our supplies, Jupiter. I'm here to blow up your damn building and get as much gold as I can stuff in my duffle. I don't run out on people."

Jupiter cringed from the comment but didn't say anything.

He hated it when Ivory reminded him and others that John T. Ivory was a combat veteran with honors. He made a vow, though, to kill John T. Ivory as soon as the job was completed. I'll never let a man talk to me that way. Ever. Self-satisfied Sergeant of Infantry will die with a bullet in the back.

"What did you learn from Conroy? What kind of schedule are we on?" Ivory asked for the second time. "Sure don't want that stuff in the shed to be discovered."

"Looks like a few weeks longer. They're talking February. The presses have arrived, and they expect bars of gold and silver to start arriving in a couple of weeks as well. Linda hasn't got those plans for us yet. I'll give her a good kick in the butt if she doesn't." Jupiter was in an awkward situation and knew it. He had good people doing their jobs and he recognized that he didn't actually have anything to do with the bombing of the mint except for the idea of it.

Each person involved was an individual, not answerable to anyone, and that frustrated the hell out of the man who desperately needed to be looked up to as the leader. He was a failure as a farmer, failure as a soldier, and only succeeded as a bank robber because of Linda Bricky and her ability to plan. He told himself over and over that he would not fail in his effort to hurt the Union by blowing up all these buildings.

No one had ever asked him why he had this terrible desire to hurt the Union. If he had taken the time and effort to think about it himself, he wouldn't be able to come up with any kind of logical answer. There wasn't any logical answer. He was angry at the Union, had deserted the Confederacy, was a failure as a man, and had to blame something or someone. Federal buildings became the answer, logic or no.

"WHAT THE HELL HAPPENED TO YOUR FACE, ENDICOTT?" Orville Conroy had been assigned to work with the stone masons and Endicott was his leader. Despite his small stature, he enjoyed the hard work, knew that he would also be the one to destroy everything he was building. Endicott frightened most men just by being near them, but Conroy found pleasure in the man's huge size and strength. The two were exact opposites of each other. Conroy, a sleazy, skinny, half bald coward and Endicott, a giant, filthy, fighter.

"Met a man who likes to fight almost as much as I do," Endicott smiled through swollen and cut lips. One purple eye was almost closed. He had cuts and nicks all over his head and face, and one hand was wrapped and bloody. "Good man. We'll drink together tonight. You'll like him."

"Can't stay out too late," Conroy said. He didn't want Jupiter screaming at him for coming home late. "The old lady don't much care for it," he lied. "Closest I ever come to bein' in a real fight was during the war. Got knocked out and left for dead. Just walked away from it when I woke up."

"I love war," Endicott said. "Bet I killed fifty of them filthy rebs. Most with my bare hands. It's okay shootin' some bastard, but grabbin' 'em and killin' 'em with my bare hands was the best."

Conroy shrunk back two steps, wanted to run, fast, far away. "Ain't never killed nothing," he almost whimpered. Endicott looked at the poor excuse for a man and suggested that he get back to work.

"I'll teach you some things after work, Orville. Hearin' bones break and men scream is good for the soul. You'll like my new friend, too. His nickname is Bull. I need a name like that, don't you think?"

Conroy already thought of the giant as a bull buffalo. "Maybe you could call yourself Buffalo," he all but whispered. "A raging buffalo."

"Ah, Orville, that's nice. I like that. Buffalo Buster Endicott, that's me from now on." It was the first time Conroy had heard that the man had a first name.

"Mr. Curry had some big ideas for this valley and the state," Slim Calhoun said. He and Irene Thorndyke had been to Abe Curry's office at Irene's suggestion. "The man actually donated the land for the state capitol building. And he's the driving force behind building the mint. That's a lot of ambition, I think."

"He bought a large chunk of the Eagle Valley when he moved here from California. Most of it is now Carson City. He's a builder," she laughed. "You had a lot of questions about how the building was designed, where the vaults were, where the coin press was. I wouldn't think that a cattle buyer would be that interested."

There were lots of questions involved in that one statement and Calhoun had to work out his answer before saying anything. "Why don't we find a quiet table and talk for a bit, Irene." They slipped across the street from the mint building site to the Palace Club and sat at one of the tables in the back.

"Guess it's time for the truth, dear lady," Slim said, bringing a couple of beers to the table. "Bull Morrison and I are not cattle buyers."

"Didn't think so," Irene said. Her eyes were sparkling, and she had a mischievous look on her face. "You're here to rob the mint? Or what?"

Slim had to laugh. "Rob? No. Keep it from being robbed? Yes. My partner, Bull, is U.S. Marshal Bull Morrison and I'm Deputy U.S. Marshal Slim Calhoun. We believe there is a gang planning to blow up the mint and steal the gold and silver when it is up and running. And, I'm telling you this in confidence, Irene. We would appreciate it if you kept it so."

"Oh, my," She said. It was almost a gasp and she quickly looked around the almost empty saloon to make sure no one heard what he said. "So that was why all the questions about how the building is being built. There's someone you might want to meet. She wanted a job here, but I don't hire women to hustle drinks or whatever else they might offer. She said she rented a small cabin to some military men but doesn't know what their business here is."

"Military men?" Slim Calhoun jumped at the comment. "Wouldn't happen to have the names, would you?"

"She said the man who paid was called Colonel Jupiter. She's never met him, a friend, Linda Bricky arranged for the rental and brought the money from this Jupiter person." Irene Thorndyke could almost feel the tension in Calhoun. "Do you know this person, Slim?"

"Afraid I do," he said. Linda Bricky is here with Jupiter, eh? So, since she was the reason most of his bank jobs were successful, this must be a robbery, not blowing up the new building. Will they rob the mint? Doubtful. Will they stop a train load of gold coins? Most likely.

Slim sat back in his chair with just the slightest smile on his face. "Curry said the mint wouldn't be operational for another two to three weeks," he said. He was talking more to himself than to Irene. "I've got to find Bull. Do you know where this house is they rented?"

"I could tell you where it is but it wouldn't mean much. Many of the streets haven't been named yet." She laughed walking to the bar for pencil and paper. "I'll draw you a map. It's about a mile west of town, sits off by itself in a large stand of pine and fir. There's a small corral, a carriage house, well, and privy."

"You seem to know it well," Slim said.

"Should. I lived there for a couple of months when I moved here." She handed him the map she drew, and he stood, kissed her hand, and headed out to round up Bull Morrison.

Best news we've had since arriving. Conroy working at the site, getting Squash to watch him, and now knowing where these yahoos are holed up. We might win this fight. It would be nice to know why they want to blow up the building. It can't be to get the coins. They're right. It's better to rob during transport.

Calhoun walked the short distance to the Virginia and Truckee Railroad depot hoping to find Bull Morrison. The train from Reno was just pulling in and Morrison was on the landing watching for Squash Monroe. "Got some good news, Bull. Squash on this train?"

"Supposed to be. Train's late. Probably because of something he did. Hope he's on it coz I could sure use a cold beer right about now."

"I'm thinkin' more a pot full of hot stew, a bottle of vintage brandy, and a fireplace, myself," Calhoun said. "These mountains act like a funnel, and this wind got its start somewhere north of Alaska. We need to wrap this up and get back to San Francisco."

"I don't mind the cold that much," Bull said. The scar on his face was a bright scarlet. "It's the wind that curdles my blood. That pot of stew sounds mighty good, Slim."

CHAPTER 6

"I'M THINKIN' SOME BAD THOUGHTS, LINDA." JOHN T. IVORY WAS IN Linda Bricky's bed on a cold morning. "Do we need Jupiter?"

"That's not a bad thought, John T. There are so many problems with the ideas behind what Patrick has for this operation that something is sure to go wrong." Linda refused to call him by Colonel or by Jupiter, insisted on using his real name. "You know he's mad, has been since his pa whupped him with a barn plank." She had to laugh saying that, then got serious again. "You and I could take out a shipment of coins without much trouble. What did you have in mind?"

"We can't walk away from him because he would cause us a lot of trouble. Can't involve Conroy. Two cowards on our tail would be bad. I tried to get Jupiter in a fight once and he simply won't, so killing him in a fight won't work." Ivory pulled her to him and enjoyed the warmth for a moment.

"We need an excuse to get him away, up in the mountains, alone, and kill the dirty bastard," she said. "What would get him away from that cabin?"

"You," Ivory said.

"No, no," she said. "Oh, no."

"You know he would trail along like a cur dog if you suggested a ride in the mountains. You know, to get some fresh air, talk about how the plans have changed, and where the main blasts should take place. Bring him to me and I'll take him out."

She rolled off him and jumped out of bed before he could catch her. She let those thoughts run rampant as she dressed and turned to him. She knew he was right, knew that Jupiter had ideas about her for some time, knew he would follow along, never thinking trap or danger. "You're right, damn it, John T. What will we do with Conroy? He almost worships Patrick. You and me, we can wait until that mint starts chucking coins like rocks in a pond, grab our share when they're transported out, but Orville Conroy ain't up to our standards, John T."

"No, he ain't. Let's worry about Jupiter first," he said. "Getting rid of Conroy shouldn't be difficult at all." He got slowly out of bed, got dressed as she got the stove lit and coffee boiling. "I'll take a ride into the mountains and find a good spot to kill the fool."

"GLAD YOU MADE IT, SQUASH," Bull Morrison said. "Damn train was so late I almost died of thirst. Cold beer's right down the street."

Deputy U.S. Marshal Squash Monroe was as tall as Calhoun and built like Morrison. His mother was from Sweden, a Viking woman who loved battle, he often said, and his father was a Sioux, Oglala, from the Black Hills. Monroe's skin was a deep bronze which made his light blue eyes gleam. He wore his reddish hair in a long braid down his back and more often than not, wore only a buckskin vest from the waist up. No shirt, but the vest's elk horn conchos were pulled together with leather loops.

"Need food, Bull. Miserable trip. Sat next to a woman who talked the entire way from Sacramento to Reno." He threw his satchel over his shoulder and let Morrison and Calhoun walk him to the hotel. "That's the mint, eh? Impressive. Substantial, too. Read your stuff on Jupiter. This Jupiter fool is a bank robber, why does he want to blow up the mint?"

"If we knew that we'd know more than him," Calhoun said. "We're dealing with an ignorant, stupid person who is angry about something. The one we fear is John Ivory. He's got a brain and is an expert with explosives. We still believe that the threat of blowing up the building is designed to throw us off." They found their way to the restaurant.

"A ruse?" Squash asked. "That makes more sense than anything I've heard so far. All of us chasing a bomber and what we should be looking for is a thief. Now we're talking," the big lawman said. The waitress came over and Squash looked her square in the eye. "Buffalo turned long on open fire. The whole thing."

She giggled. "Well, all right then, a big pot of stew. Boiling hot stew. And when I'm through with that, bring another." She laughed all the way into the kitchen wondering if the man might really eat a whole buffalo.

"I started to tell you, Bull, I think I know where Jupiter and company are living." Slim Calhoun was looking at the lunch menu scratched on a chalk board. "Irene gave me a map and I'm going to scout it out after we eat. It's about a mile or so west of town."

"Why would she know?" Bull Morrison almost growled it out. "That's interesting."

"She lived there when she first moved to town and the lady who owns it just rented it to three military men. Maybe one of them is Colonel Jupiter."

"Now we're getting somewhere," Morrison said.

"Where do I fit in?" Squash came right to the point and it brought a seldom seen smile to Bull Morrison's scarred and bruised face.

"Got you a position on the mint staff. We were going to have

you shadow Conroy but if we know where they live, that's out."
Morrison looked back and forth at his two deputies. "I'm going
to continue keeping company with Henry Honeycutt and my
new sparring partner, Mr. Endicott. Between the two of them,
I've got a real handle on the building. Endicott is a stone mason
and Conroy's on his crew. Why don't you two work together?"

"Here's what I found out from the man in charge of the
construction. This Curry gentleman is quite a character." Slim
Calhoun handed Morrison the notes from his morning meeting. "He told me things he probably shouldn't have. He doesn't
know I'm a marshal and he gave away some secrets. I wonder if
it's a habit? The mint could be vulnerable to someone willing
to blow it up."

"What we need is evidence before the fact. We can't just
wade in and start shooting, damn it," Morrison chuckled.
"Ain't the old days no more, boys. We're civilized, and so, find
out what we can bring to a judge before they try to blow the
damn thing up."

"If they're even looking to do that," Calhoun said.

"I'm getting the first shipment dates and times, and we
should concentrate on that," Morrison said. "With Ivory's
blasting background, particularly blowing up railroad trains,
the shipments have to be their real target."

"MY HEAD HURTS FROM ALL THIS, PATRICK," Linda Bricky said. She
had engineering plans for the Carson City Mint laid out on the
kitchen table. "We need a break, get away for a few hours. Do
something different."

"You're testing me, woman," Jupiter said, "but you might
have something. I'm wound tight as a clock, ready to shoot
someone. Anyone. Might take a little walk later." He was pac-

ing around the small kitchen, stuffed some wood in the stove, poured more coffee, and sat back down.

"Maybe a ride into the mountains," she said. "I think this road out front leads way up into these mountains." Ivory had ridden out a couple of hours earlier after a ride the day before. He would be waiting for them five miles or so up the road. "That would be so relaxing. Let's take a ride for a couple of hours and then come back to this."

She gave him the best smile she could, made it an invitation, and Jupiter jumped at the idea. He'd wanted to be close to Linda from the start. They had a good business relationship, but he wanted so much more. He hated that she and Ivory seemed close, that she and Conroy had somewhat of a relationship. He would take this opportunity to be close.

Ivory, as far as he knew, was rounding up fuse cord, blasting caps, and more dynamite, Conroy was on the job at the mint, it would just be Linda Bricky and Colonel Jupiter for the next few hours, alone in the mountains. *She'll never smile at Ivory again after being with me. She'll find out what a real man is.* He was having a hard time keeping himself under control.

Jupiter tucked a bottle in his saddlebags, and they rode out early in the afternoon. "I want to see that building as a pile of dust, Linda, and then we'll move to San Francisco. That building is even larger, and the Denver Mint will be last on our list. The Union will suffer."

Linda didn't say anything, just wondered what drove the man. *I'm going to be rich; John T. and I are going to be rich after you're gone to dust, Patrick Mullins. Your little war ends in an hour or so and my life with Mr. Ivory begins.* "There's a little brook up here, Patrick. We can spread our blankets and relax for an hour or so. We have to be very careful when we blow up that building. Where the presses are, where the coins will be, is vulnerable to the blast."

"Don't want to ruin all that beautiful gold," She laughed. "Well, let's think of something else for a couple of hours. Something warm, friendly, quiet." She was teasing him and could see that it was working she led him into a grove of fir along the banks of a small stream. There was thick grass for the horses and she was out of the saddle tying hers off quickly.

"Look down there," she said. "Soft grass right alongside the creek." She almost ran down the incline to the grassy area and as Jupiter started to follow, John T. Ivory stepped out from behind a large white fir.

"Hello, Patrick," he said. He held a short-barreled shotgun aimed at Jupiter's mid-section. "Nice day to die, eh?"

"Ivory!" Jupiter spit it out. "What is this? Who the hell you callin' Patrick? I'm Colonel Jupiter and don't you ever forget it." He jumped back, looked down the hill to where Linda stood, and the truth came like a flood. "You bitch," he screamed, and went for his sidearm.

The shot that echoed among the hills didn't come from his Colt. It came from two barrels of a shotgun held by John T. Ivory. Linda hid her face, but smiled, and Ivory reloaded the scattergun. Linda ran back up the hill and they dragged Jupiter's mangled body down the slight hill and shoved it under a large bush growing near the stream.

"Won't they find it? Shouldn't we bury it or something?" Linda had seen many dead men during her short career in bank robbing, but what a double-barreled shotgun does to a man is wicked. She couldn't help but shrink back from the mess.

"Don't much care if it is found," Ivory said. "Ain't nothing there that says anything about us. Besides, the coyotes and wolves will finish him off before the night is done. All that blood will draw them in like the gold at the mint has drawn us."

"That's almost poetic, John T.," she whispered. She put her arms around his neck, and he drew her in for a long kiss. "Wonder if maybe we should put these blankets to some kind of good use."

"Just us, Linda," he said. "It's just us and as much gold and silver as we can get our hands on." There were smiles on both, and he took her by the hand, led her deeper into the meadow, and started unbuttoning her dress. She helped.

CHAPTER 7

BULL MORRISON WAS AT THE BAR IN THE PALACE CLUB TALKING WITH Leroy, the barman, when Irene Thorndyke came in. "Must be quitting time at the mint, Leroy," he laughed. "You're right on time, Irene." He managed to also nod his head such as to make sure she didn't give away the fact he was a marshal.

"Nice to see you again, Bull. Is my little saloon safe?" She walked to the end, patted Henry Honeycutt on the shoulder, and slipped behind the bar. "I really don't like that kind of behavior."

"I can't say it won't happen again, but if it does, it won't be my fault," Morrison said. "Mr. Endicott and I have reached an agreement that includes buying you new tables and not getting it on with each other."

Almost on cue, Endicott burst into the saloon along with a dozen others. "Ah, Bull Morrison," he bellowed. "I've got a new name, thanks to this gentleman here. He calls me Buffalo Butch Endicott. How's that?"

"Fits you like a buffalo robe," Morrison laughed. "And who's this fine gentleman?" Bull knew it was Orville Conroy and wondered if Endicott had become part of their little gang. "Doesn't look big enough to be working with the likes of you."

"Name's Conroy. Nope, he ain't, but he is good for keeping us in tools and stones. He ain't like us, Bull. He don't want to fight, ain't much for seein' blood and bone." Endicott let out a roar and swung his right fist in a huge arc, landing it square on Morrison's head.

Morrison shook it off and drove a one-two punch into the big stonecutter. The first hit him on the chin, the second drove deep into his groin, dropping the new Buffalo Butch to the floor. All of that was followed by the blast of a forty-five just short feet from the two.

"Gentlemen," Irene said. "Gentlemen, if this happens one more time, I will ask you to leave and insist that you never come back. This is your last chance."

Endicott looked at Morrison, both men in pain, and offered a horrible attempt at a smile. The blazing red scar across Morrison's face almost glowed from the excitement of the fracas, and he tried to return the smile. "That's good," Irene said. "Now, drink your beer and no more nonsense. I won't tolerate it." The smoking revolver was waved back and forth, the green eyes blazed, but there was just the hint of a smile. She simply couldn't hide it.

Her anger was directed more at Bull Morrison than Butch Endicott, and she walked down the bar to talk with Henry Honeycutt. "Angry ladies are the prettiest," Endicott almost whispered.

Morrison noticed that Conroy had slipped out of the saloon when fists started flying and had to chuckle. "Your little friend took a hike, Butch. Didn't fancy our brand of fun."

"Ain't worth much, but he tries. Always has questions about how the rocks work to add strength to the building. Can't tell if he's sincere and tryin' to learn or not."

Morrison thought that Conroy was learning all right. Learning where to best place the dynamite. No, I've got to quit thinking that way. I'm positive this whole thing about blowing up the building is designed to draw us away from a major robbery attempt. Jupiter is a bank robber; Ivory is a blasting expert but also a bank robber. Conroy's just a hired hand, an extra gun if needed.

Morrison knew there should be another person in the gang, somebody with inside information, but who would that be. "This Conroy feller have any friends?" He wanted to ask more questions but had to be careful. Endicott acted like an ignorant bully most of the time, but Morrison also knew that his job as a stone mason indicated the man had brains along with those massive muscles.

"Tells me he has to get home coz his old lady don't like him bein' out late," Endicott laughed. "Just imagine what she must look like. Probably beats him once a week just coz she can." He whopped Morrison on the back. "Goin' for a couple of steaks, Bull. Join me?"

"Meeting with my partner. Sorry. Maybe tomorrow," Morrison said. He watched the huge stone cutter rumble out through the bat-wing doors, rubbed his sore chin, and moved down the bar to where Henry Honeycutt was perched. "Time for a little education, Henry," Morrison said. "How about a couple of beers for us, Irene, and get something for yourself. We three need to talk."

"WHAT ARE YOU GONNA TELL Conroy when he comes in tonight?" Linda Bricky asked. They were riding back from the creek, trailing Mullins' horse. "He and Patrick got along really well, and he always has something to say about how the building's coming along."

"Don't think I'll say anything," Ivory said. "We'll put Jupiter's horse up and I'll just say I don't have any idea where he is. You go on back to your cabin and I'll go to ours, and simply play dumb."

"Makes more sense than trying to come up with some kind of story." They rode together up to the outlaw cabin and Linda continued on into the town. Ivory took his and Jupiter's horse into the carriage house and put them up for the evening. He brushed both and fed them, hoping that any sweat stains wouldn't be seen if Conroy decided to check. In the cabin, he lit a fire in the stove, put coffee on, and found a bottle and tin cup. Conroy isn't smart enough to understand that Jupiter was simply a fool. Linda and I will make good partners and that means Conroy has to die.

"THAT'S THE ONE CALLED MAJOR IVORY," Calhoun said. He and Squash Monroe were tucked under some brush far back from the cabin as Linda Bricky and John T. Ivory rode up. "I wonder where they've been?"

"From the leaves and stuff on her skirts I think I know what they've been doing," Squash chuckled. "Ivory's the blast master, eh? Paperwork Bull gave me said he was damn good during the war. How did he get hooked up with this Jupiter?"

"Blowing bank safes," Calhoun answered. "Whose horse are they leading back in? Glad we're here to see all this."

"If those two were just on a little romantic jaunt I wouldn't think twice about it, but that third horse has me thinking bad thoughts." Squash Monroe edged back out of the brush, staying low, and working toward their horses. "We know Jupiter is the one who talks about blowing up federal buildings." Calhoun nodded and Squash continued.

"That woman is probably Linda Bricky and we know her as Jupiter's partner in bank robberies stretching back to Missouri. We know Ivory is an explosives expert and bank robber. Are we looking at a new partnership forming?"

"You mean Bricky and Ivory?" Calhoun asked.

"Yeah. And is it possible that three people rode out and only two rode back?" Squash Monroe mounted up. "Think we could find out before sunset?"

Calhoun was chuckling softly as he stepped into the saddle. "That would, of course, mean that Bull's theory is right about blowing up the building being a diversion. Linda Bricky is known for planning most of Jupiter's bank robberies, and she's been very good at it. If she is hooked up with Ivory, they would be a formidable pair. He has a combat history that any veteran would be proud of, unlike Jupiter and Conroy, and no qualms about killing."

They back-tracked Ivory and Bricky for several miles on the seldom used trail, riding high into the Carson Range of the Sierra Nevada. "It looks like one person rode out some before two followed," Squash said. "I think we're looking at a planned killing, Slim."

"Looks like it. Was Jupiter the one first out, or was it Ivory setting up an ambush? If we find a body old chum, we better find some evidence to link Ivory and Bricky to the killing."

"If we find a body, my suggestion would be to leave it be, find Bull, and, maybe let the local law take over."

Calhoun had to think on that for a minute. "We've been trying to keep out of their sights, Squash, but you might be right. It would put pressure on Ivory and Bricky, and sure as hell put Orville Conroy is danger. Well," he laughed, "Let's find the body first if there is one."

"Sure didn't try hiding their prints leading off the road," Squash said. "Let's tie off on those trees."

"Somebody died right here," Calhoun said. He pointed at a

large blood stain on the grass and dirt, and the empty shotgun shells. "That's a hard way to die." They followed drag marks down toward the creek and within minutes found Jupiter's body tucked in the brush.

"These are bold and brazen killers, Slim," Squash said. "That shotgun blast was from just feet away. Horrible way to die. Let's wipe out our tracks best we can and find Bull. We don't have one single piece of solid evidence linking Ivory and Bricky to this other than speculation."

They circled well away from the outlaw cabin on the way back to Carson City and tied off in front of the Palace Saloon. "I'm pretty sure that the mint building is safe," Calhoun laughed. "The contents might not be, though. We'll need to keep a close eye on Ivory and Bricky until we get enough evidence to take to a judge."

CHAPTER 8

"HAVE YOURSELF A GOOD DAY AT WORK, CONROY?" JOHN T. IVORY WAS sitting at the kitchen table in the small cabin, a tin-cup full of whiskey in front of him. "Made some adjustments in our plans. Have a drink and I'll show you."

"Where's Jupiter? They are moving fast on that building. There's all kinds of talk about starting up the presses next week. Jupiter needs to know."

"You'll be with him soon," Ivory said. He poured another cup of whiskey and handed it to Conroy. "Follow me and I'll show you our new plans."

Conroy took the cup and followed Ivory out the back door of the cabin and toward the carriage house. "I didn't know anything about a new plan. Jupiter never said anything. Where is he?" It was dark and there was a glow from lamps burning in town, a mile away.

"I think we'll be concentrating more on taking the gold and silver than blowing up big buildings. You'll have all the time in the world to discuss it with him." Ivory had a wicked smile on his face, but Conroy couldn't see that. He took great pleasure in killing a man, in leading a man to his death.

Ivory led them into the barn and as Conroy stepped

through the doorway, he was slammed in the head with a shovel, over and over again. "You like our new plan?" Ivory snickered. "I don't think Linda would approve, but there just wasn't room for you, Conroy."

The thought of all that gold being their main target now filled his head as he watched the sad little man bleed out. "Just Linda and me from now on. Gold, silver, Linda and me. I like the way that sounds."

He muscled Conroy's body across the back of Jupiter's horse and tied it tight. He saddled his horse and mounted up for a short ride into the forest where he simply untied the body and let it fall. He trailed the unloaded horse back to the outlaw cabin and did what he could to clean up the blood and gore.

"I'll get the rest in the morning and clear out. Linda and I need to know how they plan to transport those lovely gold coins out of here. I think I see train robbing in my future." He was chuckling, even out right laughing, as he stoked the fire and poured more whiskey. "Guess buying all that dynamite is gonna pay off after all."

His dreams after the War Between the States ended always featured railroad trains exploding, bridges going up in flames, but rarely ended good. He was always running, barely escaping the dreaded Union forces. He dreams now would include exploding railroad trains, but the running away would also feature great bundles of gold and the lovely Linda's arms wrapped tightly around his neck.

SLIM CALHOUN AND SQUASH MONROE slipped into the saloon and found Morrison, Irene, and Henry Honeycutt sitting at a table way in the back, isolated from most of the patrons. "Looks serious," Squash said.

"Looks dangerous," Slim muttered. They made their way through the crowd and found chairs. "Do I see a conspiracy underway? I hope so because Squash and I have some interesting information for you." He looked at Irene and smiled. She looked frightened by Squash. "This huge gentleman with me is Deputy U.S. Marshal Squash Monroe, Irene. He's damn near as dangerous as Bull. You might be buying more tables soon."

"Oh, dear," she feigned fear and worry for just a moment before laughing. "Hello, Squash. Bull has already warned me."

"I don't break tables," Squash chuckled. "I take scalps." The half Oglala, half Swedish deputy marshal said, straight faced to Irene's delight. "Found a body, Bull. Jupiter's."

"Saw Ivory with a woman we think is Linda Bricky, coming down the trail from where we found the body. Nothing other than that to link them to the killing. I think maybe it's time to bring the sheriff in on our investigation."

"Maybe," Morrison said. He turned to Irene Thorndyke, then to Honeycutt. "Tell me about the sheriff. What's he like?" He motioned for Irene to go first.

"He and I aren't the best of friends, Bull." She looked away and Henry Honeycutt laughed right out. "He's much more interested in running his girls, his crooked tables, and his gang of thieves than he is in keeping order."

Morrison looked at Honeycutt for follow up. "Sam Pasternak runs two whore houses, gambling tables, and hot springs baths out on Warm Springs Road. He's a mean bastard, has threatened to shut the Palace Club more than once when Irene wouldn't hire his soiled doves. Intimidation is his answer to just about any question." Honeycutt took a drink and got an ugly look on his face. "Many of those who oppose him turn up dead and mutilated, Bull. When stagecoaches are held up, often the descriptions of the outlaws match some of the deputies in his department."

"Or dealers at his clubs," Irene said.

Bull Morrison looked at Irene and she nodded. "He's threatened you?" She nodded again.

"He told me if I ever hired any girl that didn't work for him, I would find only ashes when I came to work the next day. He burned the Copper Queen to the ground, Bull. Killed Lady Jane Moses who operated the saloon and bawdy house."

"Certainly changes what I had in mind," Slim Calhoun said. "I was hoping we could have that body discovered and let the sheriff investigate the murder, leaving us to stop a robbery." Calhoun looked at Irene. "Did Mr. Curry give you a date for the first shipment of coins from the mint?"

"Not a specific date. He said the second week of February. One shipment to Virginia City. They'll be returning the gold and silver to where it was mined. Almost romantic when you think about it." Calhoun smiled, Morrison grumbled, Irene frowned at him. "The second shipment, the same day, to banks in Reno and across the state."

"I assume those shipments would be by rail, not wagons?" Morrison asked. Irene nodded.

"That second one would be a much larger shipment," Calhoun said. "We're talking next week, Bull. We need local law in on this."

"I know and it appears there isn't any local law. We've stayed as far away from the mint security as possible, so far. Maybe it's time to bring them in. Are they treasury people?"

"There are two levels," Irene said. "Abe Curry has site security, people to stop theft of building material, tools, and equipment. The sheriff refused his request for security, so he hired some ornery teamsters. They do a fine job. Then there are the federal security people." She chuckled. "They are far more interested in keeping the gold and silver safe."

"The way I see it, Bull. We need to have that body discovered and reported to the sheriff, and we need to meet with the federal security people. We have a lot of coordination to consider and less than a week to get it done." He looked over to Irene and Honeycutt. "Are there any local deputies that can be trusted?"

"Sandy," Honeycutt said. Irene shook her head just slightly. "Name's Tobias Ferris but everybody calls him Sandy. Pasternak fired him a few weeks ago because he's more interested in solving crimes than finding working girls for the boss."

"He's angry as hell, Henry. Told more than one person that Sheriff Pasternak should be shot on sight. He's a marked man." Irene said. "Sandy's a big man, sometimes makes his own rules as he goes along, but is basically honest."

"Sounds like he'd fit right in," Squash Monroe laughed. "Where would we find this Sandy feller?"

"He lives out near Empire on the road to Dayton. About five miles out. Has a few acres of rocks he calls a farm. I can take you there," Henry Honeycutt said. "Might be best to wait until morning."

"No," Morrison said. "We have to keep moving on this. Squash, get back up to that cabin and keep Ivory in sight. Don't mess with him unless you have to. Irene, do you know this woman Linda Bricky? She's been working with Jupiter for some time but came to Carson City well before the gang to set things up. She's a killer and bank robber."

"She's a very attractive young woman who does extra work for Abe Curry," Irene said. "I think she lives somewhere on the other side of the depot, but I'm not sure exactly where."

"There's the connection," Slim Calhoun said. "She's got all the information on dates and shipment schedules. And she is the one we believe did most of Jupiter's bank job planning. One of those shipments next week is gonna get hit hard. Ivory knows blasting."

"Well ain't that grand," Morrison said. "Squash stay on top of Ivory. Slim, find the head of federal security at the mint and bring him in on this. Don't let him forget the Marshal Service has the lead.

"Henry, can you ride with that busted up leg?" Honeycutt nodded. "Good. You and I are going to find Sandy Ferris tonight. Irene, we'll all meet at the hotel café in the morning."

Before anyone could get to the door there was some loud activity out on the main street and Slim was the first one out. "What's goin on?" He asked one of the bystanders.

"Looks like they're hauling a body down the street."

Slim stepped out onto the muddy street and watched two deputies ride past, leading a horse with a body tied across its back. That ain't Jupiter. Gotta get closer. He walked alongside the group and finally got in enough light that he recognized the bashed in skull of Orville Conroy. So, Mr. Ivory didn't want you in on the big kill, eh, Conroy?

"Out of the way, cowboy," one of the deputies said, shoving Calhoun back with his boot. The deputy was unshaven, wore filthy clothing, and was kicking everyone who got near to their parade. "Just another drunk and dead prospector. You've seen one, you've seen 'em all," he shouted.

Drunk and dead prospector? With his head bashed in like that? You ain't no lawman, Slim thought, looking for Bull Morrison, who was standing on the boardwalk outside the Palace Club. "That was Orville Conroy they were hauling in, Bull. Ivory's got it down to just he and Linda Bricky now."

"We'll let the dove lovin' sheriff handle it, Slim."

SQUASH MONROE RODE UP THE DIRT ROAD toward where John T. Ivory's cabin was, moved off the road well before reaching the cabin, and found a good spot to hunker down in the bushes and watch the place. He could see light from a window and movement inside from time to time. He made himself a nest, had his horse hidden in a stand of trees and good grass, and wanted to know more about this man, Ivory.

"Might be a good time to see what that place looks like," he said. He moved cautiously through the brush and trees, circled up and around the cabin, and came toward it from the back. It was a pitch-black night, heavy clouds scudding across empty sky, driven by a cold wind. Squash had no trouble moving right up to a window and was able to get a good look inside the cabin from off to the side.

"Movin' out, eh?" He whispered. Ivory was packing saddle-bags, but it was something else that caught Squash's eye. There were several cases of dynamite, fusing, and blasting caps piled near the back door. "That boy's ready to take a train or two out." There was a path that led from the back door of the cabin to the carriage house barn and Squash moved back from the building into deep shadows where he could see that path.

Ivory's first trip out was with blasting caps and his saddle-bags and subsequent trips brought the cases of dynamite to the barn. This must have been the cabin that Linda Bricky got for Jupiter. I wonder why he's moving out? Is he going to Linda's? Is he running away from all of this? Or has the planning gone far enough along that he's getting ready for that first shipment?

It took John Ivory well over an hour to move all the explosives into the barn and then another hour to pack them on Jupiter's and Conroy's horses. Squash slipped back to what he called his nest, packed up, saddled his horse, and was hidden in the brush when John T. Ivory led the two horses down the road toward Carson City.

"Wherever you're goin' Mr. Ivory, I'm goin' with you," he muttered.

CHAPTER 9

"CAN'T LET YOU IN THIS TIME OF NIGHT," THE MAN SAID WHEN SLIM Calhoun walked up to the gate at the mint building site. "You'll have to come back in the morning."

Slim hated to do it, but he pulled his badge from a shirt pocket and showed it to the site guard. "I'm Deputy U.S. Marshal Slim Calhoun. I need to see one of the federal officers who are guarding the gold and silver. I don't have time to argue."

The guard was almost as Irene Thorndyke had described, a burly teamster sporting a full black beard and wearing a heavy bear skin coat. He carried a short-barreled shotgun in one hand and the other hand was very close to the handle of a Colt at his side. "Ain't never met a Marshal before."

He turned and called to another guard twenty feet or so away. "Get Officer Desmond out here, Jackson. Got me a U.S. Marshal wants to see him." The guard turned back to Calhoun. "Kinda late at night to be visitin', ain't it?"

"Marshal business ain't got a time clock on it," Calhoun said, letting just a hint of smile cross his face. "Had many people try to steal stuff?"

"Not since we whupped the hell out of that one bunch. Abe Curry bought us all a cold beer after that night. Thought they could take the tools and things and sell 'em, I guess. Nope, ain't had much trouble since then."

Calhoun guessed the man would outweigh Bull Morrison by twenty pounds or more and was sure no one would be invading their building site. The other guard returned with the federal agent. "This better damn well be important," the agent said, as he strutted up to Calhoun.

"Wouldn't be here if it wasn't," Slim Calhoun said. He flashed his badge and introduced himself. "Need to have a nice long talk. Let's start with your name and position as we walk inside and get warm." There was no warmth or friendliness offered. "How many federal officers are on the site?"

"I'm Treasury Agent Clarence Desmond. What's the Marshal Service doing here?"

"If there wasn't a problem I wouldn't be here," Calhoun snapped. "Now, let's go get comfortable so we can talk." Desmond hesitated for just a second, turned, and led them into the building. Not a word was said as they moved through halls and into a large office with a pot belly stove glowing its warmth into the room.

There was a long conference table in the center of the room and two men were sitting having coffee. "Who is this, Desmond?" The man was dressed in an east coast style suit, rarely seen in the frontier west, had a pencil mustache, slicked back gray hair, and an air of self- importance about him.

"I'm Deputy U.S. Marshal Slim Calhoun. Are you the agent in charge here? If not, please get that agent now." Wonderful. They've brought Washington all the way out here. I've met these damn types so many times.

"Deputy U.S. Marshal, eh? I'm Chief Agent, Thaddeus Winston Fogarty, Western Division, U.S. Treasury, Deputy Calhoun. What possible business, have you with us?"

"Marshal Bull Morrison and I are investigating a gang of former confederate soldiers that are planning to rob the first shipment of coins from this mint, Agent Fogarty." Fogarty laughed right out.

"Impossible," Fogarty said. He looked at the others and back to Calhoun. "It would have to be shipment because this building is impenetrable. And my men will be guarding the shipments from the coin presses to the receiving banks. There won't be any thefts, Deputy Marshal."

Calhoun stiffened at the slight. "I'm here to simply advise you of the threat. Members of the gang have been employed in the building of the mint, and in the office of Mr. Curry. The original plot involved blowing up this building but that was just a ruse to keep us from investigating the planned robbery. Don't take this threat lightly, Agent Fogarty. The leader of the gang is a well- known criminal with a long background."

"Well, you've advised us. Desmond, please escort Deputy Marshal Calhoun out. My agents are more than capable of protecting the gold and silver. Good night, Deputy Calhoun."

"Now just a damned minute." Desmond had attempted to take his arm and lead him out with force. "Take your hands off me. Agent Fogarty, you need to respond to this threat, not just pass it off like this. The Marshal Service does not deal with idle threats."

Fogarty simply turned away from Calhoun and led his remaining agents out of the room. "Best leave now, Marshal," Desmond said. He did not attempt the use of any force.

Calhoun was seething when he reached the muddy street but had to stop for just a minute and replay part of the conversation. It's a damn good thing I went and not Bull. He would have torn that poor little screw into tiny pieces. He was still laughing as he walked into the St. Charles Hotel.

"Find out anything interesting?" Irene Thorndyke was sitting in the lobby, waiting for him. "You're wearing a half smile, half frown right now."

"Indeed I am. Isn't this a pleasure?" He squeezed her hand. "Will you join me for a brandy? I'm sure I need one." They walked into the hotel saloon and took a table away from the gambling tables. "Looks like a busy night in the capitol city."

"Gearing up for the start of the legislature. Money will flow for the next couple of months. I take it, it wasn't a good meeting at the mint."

"Have you met Agent Fogarty? Pompous ass. We'll get no help from that end. Have Bull and Henry returned? I'd like to meet this Ferris feller."

"I haven't seen anyone but you, and that's enough for me. Do you all have separate rooms?"

"Indeed, we do," Slim said. "Mine is on the second floor to the right." He had his arm around her waist as they left the saloon and made their way to the elegant staircase.

"U.S. MARSHAL, EH? WELL, COME ON IN," Sandy Ferris said. "Don't know what I've done to get a marshal all riled but spit it out." Sandy Ferris was big, ugly as sin in Morrison's eye, and ready for ten rounds at the drop of a hand.

"What you've done is leave the sheriff's employ," Bull Morrison said. "I'm here to offer you a little work if you've got time to listen."

"Well, damn my soul, come on in. You gonna hire me to kill that rotten Pasternak? Have yourself a seat. Nice to see you, too, Henry." Ferris had a small but comfortable cabin and they found seats around a kitchen table near the cook stove. "Got coffee and whiskey. Which will it be?"

"Both," Bull said. "It's cold out there." He sat down at the table and took the offered cup. "Don't want you killin' the sheriff. Not right away, anyway." He allowed for a little chuckle and made a vague attempt at a smile. "I see you're not married? Have no one living with you?" Ferris smiled and shook his head to both questions. "Good, we talk open like," he said.

"There's a plot to rob the first mint shipment of coins and I don't have enough people." Morrison took the offered second cup, half filled with coffee, half with whiskey. "Henry here seems to think you might be able to help. Says you're a good lawman."

"Thank you, Henry. Shame I didn't work for one." He looked Bull Morrison up and down, couldn't help spending a little time on that ugly scar that raced across the marshal's face. "I like the idea of working for a man almost as ugly as I am," he said. Morrison noticed that he wasn't joking. At least he wasn't laughing.

"Didn't take long for the outlaw element to zero in on the mint, eh? So much gold and silver pouring down that mountain from Virginia City, and now they're gonna turn it into coins that can be stole." He laughed right out. "How can I help?"

"The first shipments are scheduled for next week. One to Virginia City, one to Reno. We think one of those trains is going to be hit hard. Have you been in the area long enough to know where a robbery might take place on both routes?"

"Born in the valley, Marshal, and I know the V&T routes inside and out. Helped cut the roads. I still have the old maps we used laying out those routes and I can show you half a dozen places on both where a train could be stopped quick like."

"Well, just damn me, Mr. Ferris," Bull Morrison almost howled. He slammed the empty cup on the table and jumped to his feet. "If you'd be kind enough to raise your right hand, I'm gonna appoint you temporary Deputy Marshal Sandy Ferris." The ceremony was quick, and the bottle passed around the table without the coffee pot. "Be at the St. Charles Hotel about seven in the morning and we'll start our planning. Bring those maps, a rifle, a shotgun, your sidearm, and ammunition. You might not be coming home for a few days, so lock your cabin down tight, Deputy Ferris."

Bull Morrison's face wasn't designed to smile, but he did give it a try. Ferris's was about the same and Henry Honeycutt almost laughed as the two looked at each other and shook hands. "Thank you, Marshal," Ferris said. He patted the shiny badge on his wool vest and gouged out his best smile. "Damn, but that feels good sittin' there all shiny like."

CHAPTER 10

JOHN T. IVORY WALKED THE TWO HEAVILY LADEN HORSES THROUGH icy cold wind, back into town, across the main street, around the train station, and into a small neighborhood of cabins. Many of the town's cabins and homes came with carriage houses or small barn type structures. It was late but Carson City was a busy state capitol and everyone seemed to have different hours. On this cold, blustery night, no one paid the least attention to the convoy.

Linda Bricky had a small carriage house alongside the cabin with a pathway from her kitchen to a side entrance on what she called her barn. She heard the horses come through her yard and toward the small barn and walked out with a lamp in one hand and a Colt in the other.

"John T.," she said. "Scared me for a minute there."

"Douse the lamp, Linda. Don't need for the neighbors to see all this." He had the horses inside and the big doors pulled to in short order and Linda followed him in, leaving the lamp burning. Along with the two horses Ivory brought, there were two others in stalls.

"Looks like you have made some decisions, John T." She saw wooden boxes marked as dynamite and other items that were obviously personal belongings. "I have the stove lit and can get coffee going."

He had the horses unpacked quickly and followed her out and into the cabin. It was very small, just two rooms, a kitchen with table and chairs, cook stove, and cabinets, and the other room had a rocker, bed, and standalone closet. The wood stove was burning hot and Ivory got right up to it, watching Linda Bricky put a pot of coffee together.

"Had to do in Orville Conroy. It's just us, Linda." He said it almost casually, she thought. As if he had no feelings toward another person. Killed old Orville as he would a buzzing gnat. "It's time now to get serious. I want to see those railroad maps you have. We'll leave out of here at sunrise and set up a rough camp near where we plan to hijack the train." He was all business, cold, just hard facts, no emotions.

"That's what I've been waiting to hear, John T." She walked over to one of the cabinets and pulled some rolled maps out. "This is the route from Empire to Virginia City," she said. The map was on top of the table and was detailed. "It follows the river and then moves quickly into the mountains. Tunnels get it through the steep places and offer good opportunities for stopping the train."

What's this?" Ivory was pointing at what looked like a series of buildings and more tracks leading off toward the east.

"That area is called Mound House. The Carson and Colorado Railway branches off and leads to southern mines. Not a part of what we're talking about." She pointed at the tracks leading north. "This is the mainline of the V&T."

"Remember we're talking several hundred pounds of gold and silver coins," Ivory said. "Blowing a tunnel and stopping the train is one thing, getting away with hundreds of pounds of coins is another. We'll need a sturdy wagon and team."

"I've arranged for one," Linda said. "It's at a friend's place in Empire just east of here and on the rail line. We can get there quickly and have it loaded and on the road in no time tomorrow. It will look like we're just a couple moving out. It has hoops and a canvas cover, so with blankets and other gear on top of the coin boxes, they won't be seen if we're stopped getting away."

"Jupiter said you're the best at planning. I need some loving, we need some sleep, and we'll move out first thing in the morning."

"The lovin' part I've been waiting for, John T. Sleepin' might take place but not for some time, I'm thinkin'." She had a wonderful smile on her face as she blew out the lamp and led him into the other room. "Yep, John T., I'm just not much sleepy right now."

"THANK YOU, MR. IVORY," Squash whispered. He watched John T. Ivory move the two horses into the small barn, Linda Bricky following, and moved as close to the cabin as he dared. He tied his horse off to the side and tucked himself into some bushes. "I like dark cold nights," he murmured. The heavy bearskin robe was wrapped tight as he watched the two leave the barn and walk into the cabin. Squash eased up to what he found out was the kitchen window and had a good view of the small room.

The cabin was board and batten and Squash Monroe could hear their conversation as if he were sitting at the table with them. After ten minutes he moved quickly back to his horse, led it a full block away before jumping in the saddle, and rode fast to the St. Charles Hotel. "That's a fine plan she has put together. Hit the train, load the wagon and get back on the immigrant road and join so many others moving in both directions. Damn fine plan."

Squash put his horse up and walked into the saloon just as Bull Morrison and Henry Honeycutt arrived. "Good timing, Bull. I've got some good news for you."

"Good. I have good news too. Where's Slim?"

"Just got here. Haven't seen him." Squash said.

Bull Morrison motioned for the two to find a table, get a bottle, and headed for the hotel desk to see if Calhoun had come in yet. "Seen my partner?" He asked.

"In his room, Marshal, but I doubt he wants company," the clerk said. He had a wry smile plastered across his face and gave Bull a wink.

"He's gettin' it anyway," Morrison growled. He took the stairs two at a time and rapped hard on Calhoun's door. No answer and he pulled his revolver and slammed the butt against the door three or four times, chips of wood flying from the barrage.

"Get up, Slim, or I'm coming through the door," Morrison bawled. He could hear scrambling inside the room and re- alized what the hotel clerk was winking and smiling about. "Get dressed, both of you, and come down to the saloon. We got business to deal with." He was chuckling, coming down the stairs, nodded to the clerk, and headed for the bar. Wish I could hear their conversation right now.

"They'll be right along," he said to Squash. He poured a drink, tried his best to smile as he looked at Squash and Honeycutt. "Mr. Ferris will be here first thing in the morning, and he'll have maps of the rail system that the trains will use. What've you got, Squash?"

"Ivory and the Bricky woman will pull out at sunrise to pick up a wagon and team near Empire and move toward one of the V&T Railroad tunnels on the Virginia City route. After they blow the tunnel and rob the train, they'll move east on the immigrant road, the loot hidden under personal belongings in the wagon."

"That's about as full a report as I've ever heard in my life," Bull snorted.

"I was outside their cabin, less than ten feet from them, when they laid out the plans." Squash laughed. "I could almost smell Ivory's foul breath."

"Anybody else in on this? It's a big job for just two people." Morrison and the others stood as Calhoun and Irene Thorndyke came to the table. Not a word was said, not a chuckle or smile passed between Bull and Slim. Slim held a chair for Irene.

Morrison nodded to Slim, tried to smile a welcome to Irene, and continued. "Are there others involved?"

"Nothing was mentioned. Ivory and Linda have killed Jupiter and Conroy, and you haven't mentioned any other names." Squash looked at Slim Calhoun. "They're gonna blow a tunnel on the way to Virginia City. Just the two of them."

"Bold," Calhoun said. "I spent a total of ten minutes with the head of the mint security detail. What an ass. Thaddeus Winston Fogarty, Chief Treasury Agent, he said. Has three men with him and does not want us involved. Not interested in what we know. Fully capable of handling anything that might happen. Glad you weren't there, Bull."

"Wish I had been," Morrison said. "Henry, we need one more man. I know you want to be involved in this, but with that bad leg I don't think you should be."

"I'm going to be, Bull. Just not like you two. Have you considered your sparring partner?" Honeycutt had a twinkle in his eye and Irene laughed right out.

"Oh, dear," she said. "Poor Mr. Ivory." Everyone was laughing except Bull Morrison.

"Don't know which side of the fence he's on, Henry. He was close to Orville Conroy who was there to get information. Is he involved in what Conroy thought was going to be blowing up the building? Buffalo Butch Endicott would be a hell of a set of muscles if he was on our side. We don't have time to find out."

"We do, Bull," Calhoun said. "Squash and I will follow Ivory and Bricky out in the morning, and you and Henry find Endicott and nail him down."

"That would work." Morrison sat back, thinking. "It would work. You take Sandy Ferris with you, too. He knows that country like the back of his hand. Said he helped with the roadbed. Let's call it a night coz it's gonna get busy in the morning."

"Will you walk me home, Slim? It's kinda late for a lady to be out alone."

Slim smiled, dared Bull Morrison to chuckle or snicker, and took the lady's elbow. "My pleasure."

"Sunrise," is all Bull said, heading toward the hotel doorway.

It was a long cold walk to Irene's home. "Feels like a storm might be headed our way," she said. "Take your heaviest coat, Slim."

"Have you ridden that train to Virginia City?" She nodded with a smile. "Your maps make it look like a pleasant run. How fast would that train be going as it approached that first tunnel?"

"It's a slow climb out of Mound House, then it levels off some for the approach to the tunnel and the train picks up a bit of speed. Never that much, though. Any horse could keep up easily."

"That's where they'll hit. Sure do want to stop this before they hit but with enough evidence to send them to the gallows. We've got at least two people dead so far. Don't need more." Slim wanted to stay, Irene wanted him to stay, but duty won out that night.

CHAPTER 11

IT WAS AN INTERESTING CARAVAN THAT JOHN T. IVORY LED OUT FROM Linda Bricky's carriage house. They were on saddle horses and he was trailing two horses packed heavy for the journey to Empire. The morning was icy with a brisk wind blowing in from the north. February in northern Nevada can get bitter cold and produce some incredible storms. The mountains that cascade down into Carson City are well over ten thousand feet high and are called the Carson Range of the Sierra Nevada.

"Once we get on the highway we won't seem out of place," Linda said. She had wrapped a wool blanket over a heavy winter coat while Ivory wore a buffalo robe coat to ward off the cold. As skinny as Ivory was, there was room for two under that robe. "Just a few blocks to the highway."

Despite the early hour there was considerable commercial traffic coming from and going toward the V&T Railroad depot. The short line connected with the Western Pacific in Reno, carried gold and silver from Virginia City, and provided needed commerce to the Carson Valley. No one seemed to pay the least bit of attention to the little caravan.

Except for three men, that is. Sandy Ferris had met up with Slim Calhoun and Squash Monroe on time and the three rode to where the immigrant road moved east out of the capitol. "We could end this right now," Squash said. The others looked at him, questions obvious in their faces.

"We don't have any evidence at all," Slim said. "As far as anything we can prove or even attempt to bring before a judge, we have nothing. I don't see how we could, Squash."

"I watched him load several cases of dynamite on those horses last night." He had a twinkle in his eye. "One well-placed hot piece of lead and there will no longer be a threat to the mint's coinage. Just one little piece of hot lead."

"Tempting, Deputy Monroe, but no, not today," Slim chuckled. He turned to Ferris. "Squash heard them say they had a wagon and team somewhere in Empire. You live there, have you seen anything like that?"

"Every time I step out of my cabin, Slim. Empire isn't a neat little village of homes: it's where heavy industry lives, so wagons, teams, movement, is an all-day affair. Wheel wrights, wagon makers, rock crushers, rail line spurs, furniture man-ufacturing. Linda Bricky could not have picked a better place for them to not be seen."

"Leaves us no option then. We have to make sure that after they pick up that wagon, they head for the tunnel on the Virginia City route. They might still opt for the Reno route."

"Reno was never mentioned," Squash said. "They only talked about the tunnels and moving east on the immigrant road after the heist."

The three remained several hundred yards behind the out-laws and traveled at a comfortable walk in the cold wind. "The road will follow the railroad and the Carson River through a canyon and then up onto a plateau where the V&T will begin its northerly run into the mountains. A narrow-gauge line, the Carson and Colorado will branch off south." Ferris had worked on building the roadbed for the V&T and knew the country.

"Once we know for sure that they have a wagon and team, I wonder if we might be better off to ride on ahead and wait for them somewhere along the rail line. If we continue to just follow, will we give ourselves away?" Slim Calhoun asked.

"When they climb out of the river canyon, they would then follow the rail line and we would stand out as following them." Ferris said. "The roadway doesn't follow the railway."

"I wish that ass Fogarty hadn't been so closed mouthed." Slim was still angry at how he was treated by the federal agent. "He'll have his people locked inside that gold-filled rail car and Ivory will kill them all with explosives. We have to stop these people before they blow up the train. Arrest them for conspiracy to rob rather than robbing the train."

"My guess is, Ivory will blow the tunnel closed and wait for the train," Squash said. "Then blow the express car open if those inside don't open it for them. That would be the time to arrest them."

"Timing, timing, timing. It always comes down to that, doesn't it," Calhoun said. "If we are in the right place and our timing is damn good, nobody will die." They followed for another two miles and watched as Linda led Ivory and the pack animals up to a warehouse. The sign said something about it being a foundry.

"Find us a hole, Ferris. We're gonna look mighty foolish standing in the middle of the road out here," Calhoun said. Ferris led them to a tall building, and they rode behind it, stepped down from their saddles, and Squash took up a position to keep an eye on the outlaws.

"Looks like somebody at the foundry knew they were coming. That team was harnessed and waiting for them." Squash came to where they were waiting. "Linda walked in the building while Ivory held the horses and led the team and wagon out. He's unloading the packs onto the wagon now."

In less than half an hour, with Linda driving the team and Ivory riding at the side, they moved onto the road leading to Virginia City. The wagon bed was covered by hooped canvas and Linda Bricky looked comfortable driving the team. There were two saddle horses tied to the back of the wagon. "They must have left at least one of the pack horses at the foundry," Ferris said.

"Let's ride ahead now and look at that tunnel and the area around it," Calhoun said. "Find someplace where we won't be seen by anyone and wait our chance." There was no disagreement and Slim rode out at a lope. Squash waited and followed about fifty yards or so behind, and Ferris followed Squash, well back. They regrouped as they entered the Carson River canyon.

"One nice thing about this is, neither one of them has ever seen any of us," Calhoun said. "Just look at those clouds building to our north."

"Mornin' there, Endicott," Bull Morrison said as Butch Endicott arrived for work. "Splendid day, isn't it?"

"Good morning to you, Bull Morrison. Henry, it's good to see you, and Irene Thorndyke. You look like a committee of some kind."

"I guess we are," Bull said. "Your friend Orville Conroy was killed last night; did you know that?"

"Oh, no," Endicott said. "Not much of a hand, too many questions, but an alright guy. I'll miss the little bugger. How'd he die?"

"Let's go over to the Palace Club and have a chat," Bull said. He pulled his badge as he said it, "I'm U.S. Marshal Bull Morrison and Conroy was part of a gang looking to rob the mint. I need to know where you stand."

Endicott stood absolutely still, looked at Bull, then Henry Honeycutt, and then Irene. "Marshal, eh? Only man's ever come close to bestin' me, Bull. What do you mean by where do I stand? I'm sure as hell not an outlaw if that's what you're askin'." He bristled at the comment. "I can't go anywhere. I gotta job here. What are you talking about, anyway?"

"You answered correctly," Bull said. "Your job will be safe. Now I ask if you will join me in my hunt to get the rest of that gang? Slim and others are trailing them now. What do you say, Buffalo Butch Endicott?" He asked the question, but it was more like a challenge, a dare. Endicott stood rock still for just a moment, letting the words sink in.

You could hear the roar as far away as the new capitol building when Endicott threw his huge arms around Morrison and lifted him in the air, screaming yes in a long wolf's howl. "We'll get those bastards. Oh, sorry, Irene, didn't mean to say that."

"Heard it before, Buffalo," she smiled. There was a tinkle of laughter in her voice. "It's cold and there's hot coffee at the Palace Club."

"And whiskey," Morrison said. He led them across the main street and into the saloon. "We have to get on the road," Morrison said. "A couple of cups so I can bring Mr. Endicott up to speed, and we ride. I have a big job for you, too, Henry. You said you wanted to be involved, and you will be."

The night barman, Frank Cousins, had one customer, an itinerate salesman, half in the bag, at the bar when they walked in. Irene pointed at a table in the back and went behind the bar to get the coffee and cups. "Keep the coffee coming Frank," she smiled. She grabbed a bottle on the way back to the table.

"Henry, you and Irene need to find Abe Curry as soon as you can and make him believe what is going on. That shipment will be robbed. That train will be blown up, and that federal treasury agent Fogarty must be convinced. Can you do that?" Bull Morrison was all business despite the fact he poured a generous shot of whiskey in his coffee.

"Curry is a strong man, Bull, honest as the day is long, and knows both Irene and me well. I'm sure we can make him a believer, but Fogarty? He's a head strong, selfish, egotistical fool. He'll do whatever it is he wants to do and to hell with whatever other people tell him. We'll try, Bull."

Morrison spent the next half hour bringing Endicott up to date. He sat back and looked at the big man. "You with me?"

"I tried to beat the dickens out of a U.S. Marshal? Damn, damn," Endicott smiled. "Almost did, too. Hell yes, I'm with you, Bull. Wouldn't want it any other way. Got a problem, though. Supposed to be at work in ten minutes, but that's okay with me, but the fact is, I don't even own a horse."

"I'm sure they got a horse big enough for you down at the stables," Morrison laughed. "Let's get this show on the road. Don't let me down, Henry."

Abe Curry ate breakfast every morning at the Morning Star Pancake Parlor, which just happened to sit on Curry Street. Irene and Henry found him in discussion with one of the coin press operators when they walked in.

"Henry. Good morning. How's that leg of yours? Miss Thorndyke. You're out early this fine winter day." Curry stood as they approached his table. "This is our coin press operator, Sean Jameson."

"Good morning, Abe," Irene said. She nodded to Jameson. "We have a serious situation we need to bring to your attention. May we join you, please?"

"Of course," Abe Curry said. He and Jameson grabbed

some chairs and Henry helped Irene get settled. "Serious situation? I hope it has nothing to do with the mint."

"I'm afraid it does, sir," Henry Honeycutt said. "In the last few days, a team of U.S. Marshals has arrived in town to break up a gang that at first they thought were coming to blow up the mint."

"Blow up the mint? My mint? No, no." Curry almost cried out. He had been the driving force to get a mint built in Carson City, donated the land for the capitol, designed the mint, and was considered the father of the program.

"It was a ruse," Irene said, quickly. "The plan was, really, to rob the shipments from the mint. The first shipment is due to leave in the next day or two and Marshal Morrison is sure the train will be robbed on its way to Virginia City. He and his deputies plan to do everything they can to stop that from happening. Two people have died already because of this plan."

"The shipment is leaving tomorrow morning, Irene. What can I do?" Curry asked. "We can't stop the shipment. All the arrangements have been made with banks, express companies and security at the various locations."

"Morrison attempted to alert the federal treasury security people here about the attempt and they all but told him to get lost. They don't believe him and plan to have their people in the railcar with the coins. The gang plans to blow up the train."

"Fogarty is a proud easterner, I'm afraid." Curry said. Henry laughed right out. Curry frowned but also gave just a hint of a smile after a moment. "Let's go find the federal agent and have a chat. Mr. Jameson, will you excuse us? Thank you."

It was a quick walk on a cold and windy morning to the impressive structure, now all but finished and ready to work. Curry led them into the building and to Fogarty's office near the massive vault where the coins were stored after minting. "Agent Fogarty, I've just been informed that the federal marshal service is investigating the possibility of a robbery of our first shipment. What are you planning to do about that?"

"What makes you think the marshals would know something that the treasury department wouldn't know? We've not heard of any such thing except for the ravings of a deputy marshal late at night. Probably been drinking and wanted to make a name for himself."

"The gang is already moving toward the tunnel north of the Carson River and plans to blow up the train," Curry said. "You can't allow your men to ride inside the express car. They must be available to fight off the gang. Marshal Morrison is moving his deputies into position as we talk."

"I'm sure if my service was aware of a planned robbery I would have been notified. Our job is to protect the coins and to do that, we ride with them. I and my men will be with the shipment, and, you'll see, the shipment will get through fine. The word of a saloon girl and an injured worker certainly isn't the gospel."

"How dare you," Irene snapped. "You arrogant little snipe, you're setting your men up to be killed, and if you call me a saloon girl again, I'll have pieces of your hide on display behind my bar."

Curry was angry, too, and Henry was waiting for the real fight. "Your attitude and lack of understanding of the situation may well kill your agents, Fogarty. I plan to alert the train crew of the possibility of an attack. I also plan to send wires to San Francisco and Washington. Good day, sir."

Curry led the group back to his office. "Can't do any more than that, I'm afraid. The first shipment will leave on time, Tuesday morning, February 11, 1870, as noted on my desk calendar," Curry said. "I'll alert the train crew." He sat at his desk, drumming his fingers, worry lines spread across his face.

"Thank you, Irene, Henry. We did what we could."

"Bull won't like this, Irene. Is there any way we can get the word to him that the federal treasury agents will be locked inside that rail car?" Henry Honeycutt knew there wasn't but had to ask. "That's a level of arrogance I haven't seen since I left Virginia, years ago."

"Bull and Slim are on their own, I'm afraid," she whispered.

CHAPTER 12

"WE LOOK LIKE PILGRIMS READY TO CROSS THE PRAIRIE," IVORY JOKED, riding his horse alongside the wagon driven by Linda Bricky. "We'll stay on the main road until the rails branch off toward Virginia City. Keep an eye out for anything that looks like someone following."

"I've been trying but with the hoop covering it's hard to do. I'm glad you agreed to tie the extra horses on the back. If we need to make a run for it, they will come in handy." She was almost laughing; she was so excited about the way things were falling into place. The ride through the canyon was cold, a strong wind was driven by an onrushing winter storm whipping the river, racing through the canyon, flailing trees and fellow travelers.

The mines on the Comstock had built huge mills along the river, supplied by the railroad and wagons, and the road was congested despite the early hour and foul weather. "We'll be in snow before we reach that tunnel," Ivory said. "Miserable weather but it means there won't be many people out in the open areas once we climb out of this canyon."

"According to the maps there shouldn't be anyone along the rail line once it leaves this main road. Work crews ride the rails, there is a trail alongside the line, but rarely used. We'll be alone, John T." She had a smile on her face thinking about that. The shipment would leave Tuesday morning and that meant they would have tonight to be alone under the blankets.

She was young enough during the war that it was something the older people talked about, but old enough now that being with someone others considered valid heroes was stimulating indeed. One of the reasons she held Jupiter in contempt. He was a coward, a deserter. John T. Ivory was a hero and she would welcome him again to her blankets.

It was a few hours later when they emerged from the river canyon and climbed to the almost level plateau where the V&T met with the Carson and Colorado. "Individual riders passed us all along the way, John T., but I never saw any riders or wagons that seemed to be following us in particular. We're gonna be riding off with a lot of money, John. Where would be a good place to start spending some of it?"

Ivory laughed. He had been thinking the same thing and didn't hesitate with his answer. "I want to return to Virginia, find my pa's place and make things grow again. Ain't gonna happen, though. I'd last about three days as a farmer. San Francisco. That's my style. Fancy clothes, good whiskey, and you in my arms."

"I like that, John. There's a lot of banks in San Francisco and ain't nobody better at gettin' them open than us. Jupiter wanted to bust the mint there, but I always told him it was easier getting the money out of banks."

They rode almost casually through the throngs around the train station, where the two lines met, and followed the V&T line out toward the mountains to the north. She shielded her face from the wind and pointed north. "Can't even see those mountains." Linda was bundled tight in her wool blanket, hiding her face as best as she could.

Snow was riding the strong winds down from the Virginia Range and the tops of the mountains were covered in heavy clouds. "Snow's gonna hide our tracks too," Ivory said. They followed the rail line across the broad plain toward the towering mountains. "It'll be dark by the time we get near that tunnel. Our camp will have to be back and away just in case someone comes through."

"With a big fire," Linda quipped.

ENDICOTT HADN'T SPENT HALF the time on the back of a horse that Bull Morrison had, and the marshal had to continue keeping him moving at a strong pace. "We gotta get in front of them, Buffalo. Come on," he yelled, whacking Endicott's horse with his gloved hand.

"Argh," Buffalo would growl, but did his best to keep up. "I'm a wagon and buggy man, Bull Morrison, not some damn trail bum. Give me a parlor car on the railroad, not a hard leather seat on a pile driving horse."

"There they are," Bull yelled. "Half a mile in front." He pointed out the wagon and outrider. "We'll just ride on by. Don't give 'em a second's look. Keep your horse at a strong lope, right alongside me. We'll slow back to a walk when we're well past them."

Ivory and Bricky didn't pay any attention to the two riders as they were passed, and neither Bull nor Buffalo even glanced at the two outlaws. Bull led them up and out of the canyon at a strong lope and didn't slow down until they reached the terminus of the two rail lines. "We will be able to see where the rail line goes, but we don't want to ride alongside. We'll go cross-country, Endicott. Don't want them to know they're gonna have visitors."

"We're riding into one hell of a storm, Bull, I've seen these come raging down from the north before. I ain't much for gettin' out of towns and cities, and now you're talking about riding out cross country, no road, nothing to guide us. How we gonna find Slim and them?"

"My guess is they'll find us. Any trail they might have left will be under a blanket of snow within the hour and I'm sure they will be well away from that tunnel."

The rolling hills were covered in stunted cedar, piñon pine, and sage, slowly being covered in an icy coat of snow. They rode through open country about half a mile from the railroad track, watching for Calhoun and Ferris. It was Squash Malone who tracked them down.

"Hello, Bull." He shouted it out from behind a stand of trees. "Don't shoot, it's Squash Malone."

"Good to see you," Bull answered back. "Where's camp? Startin' to get chilly out here in the wilds. Children are miles behind us, will probably follow the rails to the tunnel."

"Camp's a couple of miles up. Slim and Ferris have a fine set up for us. We're two miles or more from the tunnel and up in a stand of rocks, hidden from view from most angles. Ferris knows this country."

They were hunched in their saddles and followed Squash Malone across the high desert and into the rocks. A large and warm fire greeted them as they rode around the standing pillars of stone. Calhoun and Ferris had a large tent erected, a lean-to covered their saddles and other gear, and the fire put considerable heat in the tent.

"It'll be close to sunset before those two get anywhere near that tunnel. We need to know exactly where they camp." Bull got right to it as he unsaddled his horse and tucked his gear away. "This storm is going to make tomorrow one miserable day. I'd like to stop this before the robbery attempt, if possible. What's your thoughts, Slim?"

Slim had busted up train robberies before, but usually while the robbery was in progress. "I said to Sandy Ferris on the ride up that it would be best if we can arrest them on conspiracy to rob, but the country itself might negate that. Rocky, steep hillsides, and very open. It would be ideal to catch them as they set the charges to blow the tunnel closed."

"I'm not sure they'll blow the tunnel closed, Slim. I'm thinking they'll blow the rails well before the tunnel, out in the open," Bull said. "We gotta plan for both, but first, we gotta know where they are."

"We got here early enough for me to do some scouting around," Squash said. "I'll ride out and wait for them, let them get camped, and come back. I've got a good lay of the land."

"Gonna be cold. Take some meat with you," Bull said. "I don't have to tell you, don't get seen and don't get caught. That Linda Bricky might be a young woman but she's a known killer and Ivory has enough paper out on him to scare most men."

Squash Malone just grunted as he stepped into the saddle. "I don't get caught, Bull. I do the catching."

"SNOW'S BLOWING AROUND so that we can see the trail alongside the rails," John T. Ivory said. "I don't see any fresh tracks at all. We're gonna pull this off, Linda. There'll be thousands of dollars tucked in the bottom of that wagon by tomorrow at this time. You got a plan for us to get out of here? You said something about using the main highway out there."

Ivory knew how to blow up bridges, railroads, buildings, but never considered such a thing as a plan. As a sergeant in the confederate army he was told what to do, when to do it, and often, how to do it. Others did the planning, the thinking. What happens after you blow up the bridge, railroad, or building was someone else's problem.

Linda Bricky had been planning bank robberies for Jupiter for several years and those plans always included how best to get away from the scene. "I've got some good maps of where the tunnel is and roads that will get us far away from here. We have to go east, but then we'll swing north and up to the highway that goes through Reno.

"John T., it might even be fun if we catch the train in Reno and let it take us to San Francisco. It might even be the train carrying that other shipment from the Carson mint," she laughed.

Ivory was riding in front of the wagon and it was slow going on a narrow trail. The rail line was starting up into the rolling foothills of the Virginia Range, heavy snow was driven by cold wind, and it was quickly turning into evening. "We need to find a good camp site, John T." She said. "It'll be dark soon. Looking forward to a hot fire."

There was no thought in either of their minds that someone might be watching or searching for then. Ivory rode at a comfortable walk and Linda kept the team in proper order. Linda Bricky was thinking of a hot fire and warm blankets for the two of them, Ivory had other thoughts creeping into his mind. Such as, "I've always been a loner, and she's so damn clingy. Don't much care for that. I need her and that wagon, though."

CHAPTER 13

"DONE THIS SO MANY TIMES," SQUASH MALONE MUMBLED, "AND NEVER have really liked it. The Indian half of me learned the art of the wilderness well, but the white side of me would rather be sitting in front of a hot fire." He was smiling, remembering how his Oglala father had raised him the Indian way. Moves Like Lion had found the beautiful Swedish Katrina Johansen, lost in the woods, and carried her off to be his wife. She never argued once.

She insisted her large first son speak the native tongue, English, and Swedish. As a family, they lived from time to time in or around towns, often in an Oglala village, and shunned the troubles that were brewing when the war between the white men was over. Katrina saw to it that Squash was well educated in language, numbers, and the concept of right and wrong as it relates to living in the white world.

"She told me wild and wonderful stories about her ancestors, the Vikings, and how they sailed the seas in small boats, captured whole cities, and plundered castles. I've never met a woman more beautiful or more exciting than my mother."

Moves Like Lion saw to it that his first son knew what was expected of a Sioux warrior, could move through the wilderness without fear, and could provide for the family. Squash Monroe took his last name from a book his mother gave him. Terrence Monroe was a pirate who only stole from other pirates, and Squash desperately wanted to be a pirate as he grew up.

It was some sense of trying to understand morals and ethics that led him into law enforcement, first on a reservation with a local Indian Agency Police, then almost forced into the marshal service by Bull Morrison. "Bull and I stood back to back, four men with knives were coming at us from every angle, our weapons were our fists and feet. Two went to their graves and two went to prison. He took my Indian police badge off my shirt and replaced it with a Deputy Marshal's."

The smile lingered as the storm raged for several hours and it was close to midnight before Squash was able to locate the outlaw camp, tucked in a draw, surrounded by stunted pine and cedar. The winds had calmed, and the heaviest snows were over, leaving several inches on the ground. As the skies cleared the cold set in with a vengeance. It was the cold that forced John T. Ivory to roll out of the blankets and feed the fire, and that is what allowed Squash to find the camp.

Squash spent at least half an hour plotting where the camp was, where the rail line was, and how far the camp was from the tunnel, and rode back to the marshal's camp. "They're only half a mile from the rail line and tunnel so Bull might be right. They might be planning to blow the rails not blow the tunnel closed."

It took more than an hour to wend his way through the snow covered mountainside and find the camp. "Better get up, Bull," he said. "We got some talking to do." The camp was up, the fire re-kindled, and coffee boiling in minutes.

"We're about three miles from their camp," Squash said. "It's in a closed draw that looks down on the rail line. The line comes around a blunt ridge and runs straight for half a mile before turning into a narrow gap and entering the tunnel."

"I helped build that section," Sandy Ferris said. "We had to make a deep cut in the mountain before actually going into the hillside. There's a sharp turn before entering that cut."

"I saw that," Squash said. "I think you're right, Bull. They'll blow the rail line along the flat and straight section. That's really open country. Anyone moving around is going to be seen for miles."

"What about coming from the other direction? Coming in from the tunnel?" Slim Calhoun was wrapped in a point blanket using a tin cup full of hot coffee to warm his hands. "Would that cut you mentioned be deep enough to hide us and still be close enough for us to hit 'em before they attack?"

"It's deep enough to hide us but not close enough to do us any good," Ferris said.

Bull had the fire built up good and sat on a bundle of blankets, nursing coffee sweetened with some rotgut whiskey. "This storm might end up being our friend," he muttered. "We're gonna have to split up. Squash, you, Slim, and Ferris work your way as close to those tracks as you can get. Wait until Ivory and Bricky have committed themselves to blowing the rail line and then take them."

"There is the chance that you can't. Butch, you and I are riding back to the station where the train will stop for water and hope we can talk to Fogarty. If not, we'll ride in one of the forward cars to fight Ivory and Bricky. Slim, either your group or mine will be successful. The best scenario is to not let them blow up either the rail line or the train itself. I think we agree the tunnel is safe from this attack."

"I think the shipment is leaving the mint about six this morning," Slim said. "Irene said the train is scheduled out at eight. We have hours to get in position. We don't want to scare these people off. These people, because of their conspiracy to rob this shipment, are responsible for several deaths already. They need to be stopped not scared off."

"WHEN WE BLOW UP THE TRACKS, John T., will the engineer have enough time to stop? I'm worried that he will stop before running off the rails and be able to race backward to the water tower for help."

"That engine will be moving fast after making the climb to this level run. I'll light the fuses so that the rail will blow as the engine arrives." Ivory said. "I'm sure there will be armed guards with the shipment, and they'll remain locked in the express car. We'll just blow that car up. Can't hurt the coins," he laughed. "If the blast don't kill 'em, we will. We need to get down there with the wagon and team as soon as we can."

"At least the storm's over. Some of these storms last more than a couple of days. I'll sit high in the wagon while you're planting the explosives, keep watch."

"No, there ain't nothing to watch for out here. I need you to help. The fuse is cut for two minutes and in the caps. I'll need you to insert the caps and bring the dynamite to me as I get the holes dug. Then we'll get you and wagon moved off and hidden. I'll light the fuses when I see the train. Two minutes gives me plenty of time to get safely back from the blast."

She wanted to argue that a close watch was needed. Anyone could be riding through the area and spot them. Even a railroad work crew could be around, maybe because of the storm. She made up her mind that, even if he didn't want her to, she would keep a close watch on the area around where they were working.

"I'm going to use two sets of five sticks each, one on each side of the tracks. That'll stop 'em for sure. We'll need another set of five sticks for the express car. The coins should be in wooden cases and will weigh a lot. Be ready to bring the wagon as close to the express car as you can."

That was another worry she couldn't get out of her mind. What would these horses do when all that dynamite exploded? Could she hold the team? What about the horses tethered to the back of the wagon? Would there be a fire to keep her from getting in close? John Ivory had done this many times during the war, Linda Bricky had never seen an explosion.

"IF I CAN HOLD UP THE TRAIN at the water tower I will, Slim, but don't bank on it. Let them make a definite move, one that will stand up in court, and nail their butts. Butch and I are off. Give 'em hell." Bull Morrison yelled as he and Endicott rode off in mixed sunshine for Mound House. "I know we'll have to ride that train in, Butch. I know how good you are with your fists. How good are you with rifles and pistols?"

"I did some buffalo hunting a few years ago. If they ain't running too fast I can nail 'em." That brought a laugh from Morrison. "Ain't never shot at a person, though."

"Try to remember that if you don't kill these two, they will kill you. Hopefully it won't come to that. Slim and Squash are a good team and we should find those two in chains when we arrive. A lot of people might die if we mess this up."

The ride back was much more pleasant than the ride out the day before. The storm blew itself out, the sun came out, and the air was almost warm as they rode into the rail complex. They found the station master, Stanton Small, and laid out the problem.

"You sound mighty sure of yourself, Marshal. I've had two wires this morning, one from Abe Curry, and another from

Thaddeus Fogarty. Curry's tells me what you're telling me. Fogarty says the opposite. What can I do?"

"That fool Fogarty is going to have his security people locked in that express car and Ivory is going to blow them all to hell. Damn him." Bull Morrison was left with just the one thought, to ride near the front of the train and try to keep it from being blown apart. "Me and Buffalo Butch are going to have to ride as close to the engine as possible. If it's possible, can you keep the general passengers off the train? We sure as hell don't want dead passengers."

"This isn't a mixed run, Marshal," Small said. "It's all freight. If you want to ride, you'll have to ride in the engine or the wood car. I can arrange that, but it'll be a cold ride."

"We'd be able to see best from the top of the wood pile, Butch. You up to it?"

"Damn right," Endicott said. "I fight best when I'm cold. I'm always angry when I'm cold. I'm angry right now." Small had to step back, looking at Endicott's face filled with a fierceness that would frighten a wolf.

"Aim it at Ivory and Bricky," Morrison said. He wasn't up to another five rounds with the stone cutter, and the smile that etched its way across his scarred and ugly face showed itself.

The train arrived on time and while they took on a full load of wood and water Morrison walked down to the express car and banged on the sliding door. "Fogarty," he yelled. "This is U.S. Marshal Bull Morrison. We need to talk. Open up."

"Not doing it. Got a wire from treasury agents in San Francisco that there haven't been any threats of a robbery attempt. This shipment is safe."

"You're a lying fool, Agent Fogarty. The outlaws are already in position to blow this train to hell and back. I'll do what I can to save your worthless life because it's my job, Fogarty. As you said, your job is to protect that shipment. You ain't protecting nothing locking yourself away from instead of stopping this robbery. You're a fool."

"My agents are in position to stop this attempt. For your sake, I hope they do. So long," he yelled. It was an angry Bull Morrison who jumped onto the engine as it began its run to Virginia City on the long, steep, climb. In the sun it was almost warm, but with the train moving, that air was bitter cold.

"How do," he said to the engineer and fireman. "I'm Marshal Morrison. Did Small tell you why we're riding with you?" The engineer nodded. "Good. If you see me and my partner there jump, or if I have time to yell at you, jump."

"Ain't never had a robbery on this line, Marshal. Hope you're wrong." The engineer was talking to Morrison but had his eyes out on the tracks before him.

"I wish I was wrong, but the outlaws are already out there waiting for us. Don't hesitate when I yell jump."

The engineer and fireman nodded, looked at each other in disbelief, and went to work. Morrison climbed onto the wood pile for the short ride up the hillside. "Fogarty's a simple-minded fool, Endicott. Well, let's see what we can see. Engineer said it's about fifteen minutes or so to that tunnel."

"I've worked with rock most of my life, Marshal. Blasted in quarries and worked great slabs of granite. If a charge of dynamite goes off under that steam engine, it will cause a secondary blast that would rip this train to shreds."

"I know, Butch. I hope we see them in time to jump. If I say jump, don't hesitate," he said for the second time. Morrison didn't chuckle or laugh, and Buffalo Butch Endicott knew the man was dead serious.

CHAPTER 14

THE ROLLING FOOTHILLS GAVE SLIM, FERRIS, AND SQUASH A LOT MORE cover than Squash thought they would have as they left their camp and moved toward the tracks. It was bitter cold but the sun was melting the snow fast. "I think our best bet is to work our way toward the flats from the north," Calhoun said. "If we come from the north and from the west side of the tracks, we're more likely not to be seen."

Squash pointed to a blunt butte to the north. "They are in a draw at the base of that ridge. We can move over the ridge and stay well east of the draw before working toward the tunnel. Should be well out of sight."

"That would lead us toward the cut we made for the tunnel," Ferris said. "A little higher up this mountain side and you run into great stands of rock and steep climbs."

Riding through snow covered sage, around pine, spruce, and stunted cedar, the three men slowly worked their way around the outlaw camp and dropped into the long cut that led to the tunnel. They worked their way out of the cut to the west and moved down the hillside toward the flat area.

"Let's tie the horses at the bottom of that rise and slip under the pines at the top," Calhoun said. "Should give us an excellent view of the rails and keep us hidden." They rode to the bottom of the rise and tied off, and taking blankets and an army telescope, scrambled to the top.

"See for miles up here," Squash said, settling under an ancient piñon tree. "They'll be coming toward the tracks from over there," he said, pointing off to the northeast. "See that little swale where the roadbed has been built up? That's where I'd lay a charge."

"We really can't make any kinds of plans until we see them," Calhoun said. "I think you're right about that raised roadbed. They haven't had time to do any looking around, though. They might just ride up to wherever and set their charges. How much dynamite do you think they have with them?"

"About three or four times more than they need," Squash laughed. "Remember, they were planning to blow up the mint. They have cases of it, lots of fuse, and plenty of blasting caps. Ivory is a pro and has the medals from old Jefferson Davis to prove it."

Calhoun stood up. "Time me on this, Squash. I don't want to take any chances." He took off at a fast run down the hillside, dodging trees, leaping over sage, and slip-sliding in the ice. He reached the horses and looked back up. "How long?" He yelled back.

"About a minute, Slim. It would be another couple or three, maybe more, out to where they would be setting their charges."

Slim Calhoun climbed back up the rise and got under a tree. "Cuttin' it close, Squash. We can't wait for them to finish laying the charges. When they start is when we gotta start. It might mean a pretty good fire fight."

"I know this area well, Slim," Ferris said. "Look along the tracks and you see rises like the one we're on, on both sides of the line. That flat area in front of us has to be the best location for them. It gives them a clean area for a getaway."

"I think he's right," Squash said.

"All right, but let's be ready to move just in case. Once we spot them, we have to get close enough to stop them before they blow the tracks. We need to be rifle close."

"You're the boss on this, Slim. Are we looking for prisoners?" Squash Malone knew the importance of bringing criminals to justice but was also aware of just how dangerous that can be.

"We want them alive if at all possible. We want to preserve as much evidence as possible. We don't want them blowing up all the evidence, we would rather not have dead outlaws. What they've already done are hanging offenses but it's best if the court hangs 'em."

IVORY RODE OUT, LEADING LINDA AND THE WAGON. "Remember that flat area about a quarter mile or so from the tunnel cut? Bring the wagon right up to the rails." He rode on ahead to do some scouting, looking in particular for signs of other people in the area. The air was crisp, the ground frozen, but the snow was melting from the abundant sunshine. If it stayed like this he knew they would be fighting mud on their getaway and hopefully not fighting bullets.

Linda Bricky drove the team slowly out of the draw and down the slight rise, out to the flats, looking in every direction for visitors. She was a good teamster, having learnt on her father's farm, and drove the team around most of the obstacles. Thoughts of a wagon load of gold and silver coins floated through her mind. She saw double eagles, eagles, and half eagles cascading through a mist of silver cartwheels and couldn't wipe the smile away. How much money will we have, she wondered, not being able to picture a large wooden case filled with twenty-dollar gold pieces.

"San Francisco," she sighed. "I've thought of that city so often. Mansions on the very tops of hills, a bay filled with ships from around the world, and banks overflowing with money, just waiting for me. I tried to explain all that to Patrick Mullins and all he could think about was blowing up buildings. John T. Ivory isn't a short-sighted fool."

It was such a big world, she thought, and with thousands of dollars at her disposal, it was open to her. "I'll dance in elegant gowns, shop in the finest stores, and John T. Ivory and I will rob the richest of the banks." She was almost laughing in her gaiety on the bright sunny morning.

She drew the wagon up alongside the rails where Ivory was standing, waiting for her. "Help me get these cases opened," he said. He dropped the tail gate and started moving cases of dynamite, fuse, and blasting caps. She got the cases opened, left them on the wagon, and he grabbed a pick and shovel.

"Crimp a cap onto a fuse and drive it into a stick as I showed you. Then use that fused stick of dynamite as the middle stick and surround it with four sticks, then tie them together. Make up two bundles for me while I dig the holes. The way the rail bed is raised here is perfect. I'll blow that engine ten feet in the air," he laughed.

"No, wait," he said. "Make me four bundles. I'll need two more for the express car. Whoever is inside guarding the coins won't much enjoy that show." He walked the short distance to the tracks and found an area between two ties that was soft enough to dig easily. "When I first see that engine is when I'll light the fuses. With two minutes of fuse, that'll give me plenty of time to get far back from the blast."

While Linda Bricky was seeing life in the city, diamond and ruby jewelry, and the bank's money in her purse, John

T. Ivory was seeing railroad tracks, engines, and body parts flying through the air. How many Union trains, trestles, and stations did he blow up during the war? How many people did he blow to smithereens? He loved every second of preparing a blast, almost as much as he enjoyed being wrapped in a blanket with a warm woman.

She wants to go to San Francisco and rob banks. That ain't for me. Robbin' banks is okay for people like Jupiter and Linda, but it ain't the same as blowin' up trains. I'm going to Colorado, New Mexico Territory, maybe even back to Texas. Me and two others and we can rob trains and live high.

"How deep do you put the dynamite, John T.?"

"Want it at least two feet down. The rails are bolted together with fish plates and I want five sticks right under a set of those plates. One set of sticks on the west side, one set on the east side. When you get the bundles tied off for me, get that team and wagon at least a half mile away and tied tight to some trees. Best if they're looking away from the tracks."

That answered at least one of her questions. "When you see the blast, start bringing the wagon back but don't get too close. I'll still have to blow up the express car."

She reloaded the wagon and closed the tailgate before climbing up to the seat. "Be careful, John T." She said. He had a wicked grin with his nod back to her.

"YOU SURE PICKED THAT ONE RIGHT, SQUASH," Calhoun said. They watched John Ivory ride over the rise half a mile from the tracks and shortly after, Linda Bricky with the wagon and two saddle horses tied behind. "Coming right to where you said they would."

"That's a lot of open space between us and them," Ferris said.

"Ferris, you drop down off this rise, grab your horse, and ride as hidden as possible toward the cut. Then work your way back along the track. Get as close as you can get without being seen. When you see or hear me attack, come on like a mama bear to the kill."

"Squash, you go the other way and do the same thing. I'm going to work my way through the rocks and brush and get as close as possible. I'll begin the attack with a howl and a shot into John Ivory. Any questions?"

"Not from me," Ferris said. He slapped Calhoun on the shoulder and eased away from the two and moved down the slope to the horses. Squash just nodded and slipped out as well. Calhoun gave the two of them several minutes and worked his way down the slope as well. He didn't worry about noise, only about being seen, and that meant he spent as much time on his belly as he did on his feet.

The ground was rocky, filled with low brush, a few pines, and considerable snow and ice. He could hear Ivory slamming a pick into frozen ground, could hear the shovel digging in, and then heard Linda Bricky drive the team off.

Back on flat ground, Calhoun knew where Ivory was working but couldn't see him. He kept low, moving from sage brush to sage brush, getting down on his belly and crawling when he had to, and found himself about twenty-five yards from the laboring outlaw. He watched Linda Bricky off in the distance pull up behind a stand of trees.

"Gotta remember exactly where she went with that wagon. Lots of evidence in that buggy. Come on, Ivory, plant that dynamite and I'll shoot you sure as hell." Calhoun was on his belly under a sage brush, his rifle aimed at the bad man. "Come on, plant it."

Ivory had the two bundles placed near the deep holes under the rails and eased the first bundle down, filled the hole, and tamped it with the shovel. He moved to the second hole, and as he eased it in, he heard the train coming on, fast.

"Damn," he said, and reached for his box of matches. He was lighting the second fuse when Calhoun howled out a warning, pulled the rifle up and fired. Ivory felt the bullet rip through his jacket, rolled to the ground, and down off the raised bed. Both fuses were lit and he heard the engine coming on hard.

It was the sound of pounding hooves that startled the outlaw. Linda Bricky was driving the team hard, pulled them up and the wounded Ivory crawled over the boards and fell into the bottom of the wagon. Bricky had the team at a full gallop in seconds. Ivory had his rifle up and was peering over the side of the wagon, watching Calhoun.

Calhoun was on his feet racing toward the rails but pulled up. He saw Ferris coming fast from the north and Squash from the south. Did they know the fuses were lit? He tried to wave them off when he felt a bullet tear into his arm. Ivory was shooting from the wagon and got lucky with one shot. Calhoun was thrown to the ground by the bullet, recovered his rifle and couldn't get it to his shoulder.

Ferris saw the trouble and turned his horse to the east and raced toward where Linda Bricky had driven the wagon. It was Squash who recognized the trouble Bull Morrison and Butch Endicott were riding into. He pulled his horse up short and fired two quick rounds at the train's engine.

"What the hell?" Bull heard the bullets bounce off the steel and found the source. Squash was waving his rifle, pointing ahead, and doing what he could to get the engineer's attention. Morrison jumped into the engine cab and screamed for the engineer to hit the brakes. "Lock 'em down and jump," he howled.

The engineer, fireman, Butch Endicott and Bull Morrison

leaped from train as it skidded along the iron rails. Ivory saw them and started shooting, but the distance and bouncing wagon kept him from hitting anything. The four men, covered in ice and mud, some blood, rolled as far away from the tracks as they could.

Calhoun's right arm and hand were useless, and he struggled to get the big Colt out of its holster, cocked, and pulled down on the wagon but held up knowing it would just be a wasted shot. Morrison and Endicott started racing toward Calhoun and he screamed at them. "No!" He pointed at the ground, let his hand indicate an explosion, and Bull pulled up.

"Run," he hollered at Endicott. They raced back to where the engineer and fireman were cowering near a lonely tree. "Get down," he yelled. The train was almost stopped, directly over where the dynamite had been planted, and the blast lifted the engine right off the tracks. It also ruptured the working parts of the big steamer, which increased the force of the blast by several notches.

Debris was flung out and up in every direction and came down in flames. Calhoun was blown back, tumbling through the open desert, stunned. Squash felt the blast but was far enough back that he wasn't hurt. He took refuge quickly under a boxcar as flaming and hot debris fell. The engineer was pulverized by a large chunk of hot steel, but those near him were not hit. No one could hear a thing for several seconds.

"Take care of whoever needs it," Morrison yelled at Endicott and ran toward where he saw Slim Calhoun fall. "Get Squash to help." The debris field was wide, fires burned everywhere, and Morrison had a hard time threading his way. It was several minutes before he was able to find Calhoun, laying in a puddle of blood.

"Can't move, Bull," he said. His teeth were clenched in pain and Bull could plainly see where the bullet splintered his deputy's right arm. Worse, a large chunk of hot metal had Calhoun pinned to the ground, spread across his lower torso. "Get if off before it burns me in half," Slim cried. "Hot."

Morrison ripped his jacket off and used it to protect his hands as he lifted the heavy piece of sheet metal from Calhoun. He flung it to the side and got down on his knees to find out just how much damage had been done. "Gotta get you back to town, Slim. Right away."

"Sandy Ferris is chasing Ivory and Bricky. They're in a wagon but have saddle horses tied to the back. Better get Squash on the chase. When you get Fogarty out of the express car, smash him one for me," Calhoun said. He was in a serious condition and Morrison wasn't ready to move away from him. "Go, Bull. We've got 'em dead to rights."

"You first, Slim," Morrison said. He wrapped his deputy in his now burned jacket and picked him up as if he was a sack of grain, threw him over his shoulder. He ran to Calhoun's horse and rode fast back toward the burning wreck. The first three freight cars were off the tracks, two of them burning furiously.

CHAPTER 15

WHEN THE ENGINEER HIT THE BRAKES, THE FIVE MEN IN THE EXPRESS car were thrown to the floor, cases were toppled, and one of the kerosene lamps broke into pieces, spreading the flaming liquid across the wooden floor of the railcar. "Get that fire out," Fogarty yelled.

Fogarty was splayed out on the rough floor, a case of silver coins pinning him down. "Get this case off. Gotta get those doors open before we fry. What the hell was that engineer doing to cause this?" The idea of a train robbery still hadn't registered in the pathetic easterner's mind. Smoke billowed as the floorboards caught and burned hot, and the chaos of men and spilled cases of gold and silver got in everyone's way.

Fogarty had four treasury agents with him in the boxcar and it was Desmond who pushed the heavy case off the security man. "Have to get those doors open," he said again. He worked the heavy keys in the locks as fire spread through the wooden railcar. The doors slid back and the five men tumbled out just as Bull Morrison rode up, carrying the wounded Slim Calhoun.

"A lot of help you were," Morrison snarled. "Take care of my man, Fogarty. I'm holding you responsible for this mess." Squash Malone rode up and grabbed Calhoun's horse, which was trying to shy away from the flames. Morrison jumped in the saddle and yelled at Endicott to catch up when he could. He and Squash rode off in pursuit of Ivory and Bricky.

"Is he hurt bad?"

"Smashed his arm and bleeding bad, Squash. He's tough. Let's make these bastards pay hard for this."

"THERE'S ONE COMING FAST BEHIND US, LINDA. I'm shot up bad. Find someplace where we can fight whoever was back there. Can't be caught. Push the horses hard." He was babbling and she knew he would soon be useless in a fight. Jupiter did that to her once, also. Got shot and couldn't fight and she had to do it all.

"It's always that way," she howled in frustration. "Leave me to save your skinny butts. Well, mister explosives expert, hang on," and she whipped the team in a frenzy. Sandy Ferris was riding hard to catch up, knew Ivory had managed to climb in the wagon but was not aware how badly he was wounded.

Bricky's mind, early that morning, was full of San Francisco, mounds of gold coins, and banks ready to be opened and pilfered. It's all gone. All that gold still in the boxcar back there. My man, just another loser, bleeding to death in the back of the wagon. Her thoughts were on what was supposed to be, and she had to wrench them back to what was happening.

"Where did these people come from?" Linda Bricky's mind was whirling with questions as she drove the team across the broad plain above the Carson River. "More than one man. Ivory shot one. I saw that. Then who is it chasing us now?" She couldn't get the thought that someone had given them away out of her mind. "But who?"

"Hope somebody back there saw me ride after these two," Ferris snorted, pushing his horse hard. "Gotta at least keep them in sight until I get help. Ivory has a rifle and I heard Calhoun say that Bricky was a good shot."

They were generally headed east through rolling hills. He knew there was a deep cut just a few miles in front where the Gold Canyon brought Gold Creek to the Carson River. "If that doesn't slow her down, nothing will."

Ferris was still more than a hundred yards behind the wagon and Linda was driving the team as if she were on a well graded gravel road. The rocks and brush were hit hard, wheels bounced high in the air, horses fought to stay in balance, and she never let off the whip. The off horse tripped over a sage and the front wheel hit a large rock at about the same time.

The wheel splintered, the horse fell, bringing the second horse down with him, and the wagon careened wildly before rolling over, throwing Bricky, Ivory, and several hundred pounds of dynamite, half a case of blasting caps, and a full roll of fusing into the desert dirt.

Ferris pulled up quick and jumped from the saddle, leading the horse toward a stand of pine trees. He had no way of knowing whether either of the outlaws was alive, unconscious, or waiting for him with drawn weapons. He tied his horse off and got down as low as possible, making his way toward the wreck.

He was close enough that he could hear one of the horses screaming in agony, saw some debris still in the air from the wreck, but couldn't see either Bricky or Ivory. "They're armed, Ivory looked to be hit, and they can't get away," he muttered. He saw the two saddle horses still tied to the upturned wagon and crept toward them. "If they're moving, they'll want those horses."

He was still some ways off when he saw Linda Bricky get to her feet and wipe her hands on her pants leg. She was looking around, probably searching for Ivory, saw him, and ran to him. "Good, little lady, thank you," Ferris muttered. He crawled toward a large sage brush and watched her kneel down next to the wounded man.

Ferris had worked for the ignorant Carson City Sheriff for two years and had never run into a situation like this. He could yell out that he was there and for them to give up. He could crawl up closer and demand they surrender. He could hope that someone at the train saw which way he took off and followed.

"Morrison named me Deputy U.S. Marshal," he almost laughed. "It's time I acted like one, I guess." He kept as low as he could and quickly moved toward the two outlaws. Bricky was busy tending Ivory's wounds, and there were many. Calhoun's bullet ripped through his upper right shoulder blade and the tumble from the wagon caused a severe gash to his head and what might be a broken leg. He was unconscious and his breathing was sporadic.

Ferris was almost close enough to yell out at Bricky when she spotted him. She jumped to her feet and tried to grab her rifle. "Stop!" Ferris was on his feet, his rifle pointed at her. "Stop right there and you'll live," Ferris yelled. "Stop or die," he commanded when she didn't stop.

She had the rifle halfway up, cocked, and pulled the trigger. Ferris was blown back several feet from the force of the bullet ripping through his hip. He got his pistol out and fired one shot before he passed out. He didn't know that the bullet hit her in the leg, knocking her to the ground.

"Somebody's shootin' at somethin'," Morrison yelled as he and Squash Malone drove their horses to the cloud of dust still lingering in the bright sunshine. They rode hard, seeing the overturned wagon, and finding Ferris unconscious. Bricky had crawled under the wagon and was trying to get the bleeding stopped from her leg wound.

She watched in horror as the two lawmen jumped from their horses, rifles in hand. "Damn you, John T. Why couldn't you have done your job right? I always have to bail you men out. Always," she growled, tying off a bandage on her leg. She grabbed her rifle and levered a round in. She was looking for the two men and couldn't see them.

"Rifle," Morrison said, hearing Bricky cock hers. They hit the ground, bringing their rifles up and ready. "That's one hell of a wreck. Both those horses need to be put down, Squash. That squealing hurts me clear to my soul."

"Look to the left of that wagon, Bull. That's a busted-up case of dynamite." Squash Malone eased up on an elbow and yelled out. "Give it up, Bricky or I'll put a bullet into that case of dynamite you're almost sitting on. Throw those guns out and crawl out where we can see you."

Panic struck fast as she looked around and saw the explosives less than ten feet away. She couldn't get away. The wagon was upside down and she couldn't get under it, couldn't get around it without being one big target, and remembered what Ivory had told her about one of his jobs during the war when he was trapped.

"Come and get me," Bricky hollered out. I can't get away but I can take them out with me. She crawled as close to the wagon as she could get and took a long aim at the broken case of dynamite. Come on boys and we'll all go together. So long, John T.

"It's a trap," Morrison said. He was working on getting the hole in Ferris's hip patched up. "She'll let you get close and shoot into the explosives sure as I'm Bull Morrison."

"Talk to her, Bull, and I'll crawl around and see what I can do. Don't get her all riled up and get me all blowed up," he chuckled. He snaked his way through mud, ice, and debris from the wagon until he had a clear look at Bricky. She couldn't see him, hidden as she was under a wheel that was half blown apart.

"Sure rather take you in alive, Linda," Bull Morrison yelled out. "Ivory isn't dead, is he? Both of you can live. Just throw that rifle out and crawl out behind it."

"Go to hell," she screamed. "Who are you?"

"I'm U.S. Marshal Bull Morrison and I can guarantee you won't be shot. Now, come out of there and end this. It's cold, woman."

It was and she could feel it deep in her bones. Her leg ached from the bullet wound, her head hurt from being thrown to the ground, and she didn't want to die. The wind had picked up, clouds scudded through the sky, and she was, not just trapped, but wounded and trapped. I ain't goin' to no prison, and John T., you're goin' to go to hell with me. She raised the rifle and took long aim on the case of dynamite. Squeeze the trigger and it's all over. All I wanted was to wear silk and pretty dresses in San Francisco.

The bullet smashed into her hand blowing the rifle away, blowing debris deep into her face, knocking her to the mud. Within seconds strong arms jerked her out from under the wagon, and had her hands locked behind her.

"Come on, Bull. I got her but she's a fightin' tiger." Squash was trying to dance away from kicking feet, scratching fingers, and a foul spitting mouth. "To hell with it," he said, and smashed her across the side of the head with his rifle. "That's better."

"Move her back with the horses, Squash. I'll get Ivory. We gotta get away from here. That fire's gonna hit blasting caps and dynamite sure as I'm standing here."

Before Bull Morrison moved John T. Ivory, he walked up to the two injured horses still in their harness and put them out of their misery. "Least I could do for you, boys. I'm sorry." He went to the back of the wagon and untethered the saddle horses, grabbed Ivory by his coat collar and brought the bunch to where Squash stood over Bricky.

"She alive?" He dumped Ivory next to her. "He is. Or was when I grabbed him. Let's keep 'em alive and head back to the train. Hope somebody rode into Mound House to alert them."

CHAPTER 16

"See what you can do about him, Desmond," Fogarty said. They were standing next to the unconscious Slim Calhoun. "I'm going to have a talk with that engineer." Fogarty started to walk off down the tracks. Desmond took one look at Calhoun and knew he needed a doctor and soon. "He needs medical help, Fogarty. You can't just leave him on the ground like that. He's a United States Marshal who just stopped a major assault on our shipment. He needs help."

Fogarty spun around, glaring at the deputy. "See to it then," the treasury agent said. He started to say something else, thought better of it, simply turned, and started to walk off. The level of arrogance was almost more than Desmond could handle. More than once during the last few years building the mint, Desmond wanted to smash the arrogant man, but also wanted to keep his deputy job.

"The least you can do is help me get him away from these fires, maybe under that pine over there." Fogarty motioned for deputy Sam Arnold to help Desmond, and stormed off, wending his way through tumbled and wrecked freight cars, twisted track, and numerous fires that would soon consume most of the debris. Billowing black smoke filled the air.

Butch Endicott and the train's fireman were huddled under a pine tree when Fogarty arrived. "Where's the engineer?" Fogarty snarled at Endicott.

"Dead, Agent Fogarty. He's dead. Where's Marshal Calhoun? He was shot during the attack." Endicott was treating the injured fireman, who had taken a blow to the head and was bleeding in other areas as well.

The truth was finally seeping into the federal agent's head. This wasn't an accident. The train had been attacked. Fogarty looked back down the length of the wrecked train and saw the express car fully consumed in raging fire. The coins he was supposed to be protecting were surely melting in the inferno.

Hundreds of twenty-dollar double eagles, ten dollar eagles, and five dollar half eagles, lost on his shift, gone while he was on duty, destroyed under his care. His knees buckled and he reached out for Endicott before he collapsed. "My God," he moaned.

Endicott flung Fogarty's arm aside and let the man fall to the ground. "Where's Calhoun? Answer me you twit." Fogarty simply pointed down the track and Buffalo Butch Endicott took off at a full run, a sight that would bring fear to a strong man.

"Is he alive?"

"He is, but he needs help," Desmond said.

"I need a horse. Gotta get him back to the train station. Are there any horses?" Endicott looked around, frantically, and couldn't see one. Because of his work in quarries and with massive pieces of rock, he had been close to many seriously injured men, knew the basics of treating wounds and broken bones.

Despite his public image of a barroom brawler, Butch Endicott was filled with empathy for injured and wounded people and animals. Kittens, puppies, horses, even those he brawled with, got immediate attention if they were hurt bad.

I hope a bullet wound isn't very different from a deep cut from a broken steel. If you're there, God, don't let me kill this good man.

Endicott knelt down next to Calhoun and looked up at the two treasury deputies. "Get word back to the station that we need medical help up here that the train was attacked. U.S. Marshals are chasing the attackers. One of you move now," he threatened and almost chuckled when Sam Arnold turned and ran off at a lope.

"Get me water and rags," Endicott said to Desmond. "Come on Slim, I'll do my best, old man." He got clothing, mud, and debris wiped from the wound, cleaned it the best he could and waited for Desmond to bring him the water and rags. Calhoun moaned a couple of times when Endicott touched the wound.

As big as Butch Endicott was, at this moment his touch was that of velvet as he cleaned away the mess the bullet had made. His massive, gnarled and callused fingers were gentle, almost soft, as they wiped away the filth of the desert.

Desmond returned with what he could find. "The water's from the engine. It's very hot, and these rags are the shirts from the engineer. The fireman helped me get them."

Endicott had the wound cleaned out, the bleeding stopped, and a bandage wrapped tight when Bull Morrison, Squash Malone, and the injured Sandy Ferris along with the two wounded outlaws came riding up. The injured were laid over the saddles. "How is he?" Bull yelled it out as he jumped from the saddle. "Gonna live?"

"He's a lot better now," Endicott said. "How's Ferris? Doesn't look good from here."

"Took a hit in the hip. He's hurtin', but he'll live. We gotta get these people to a doctor."

Bull Morrison was furious when he found out that, despite the warnings of an attack on the gold shipment, the treasury agents didn't bring along horses in case they had to chase the attackers. "What kind of cave does that man live in?"

Morrison was pacing around letting his anger build. "I've got four seriously wounded people here." He looked at Desmond, as if it was his fault. "Two of 'em are outlaws and two aren't. I've only got two extra horses. I don't have time for compassion, I've got to save my people before the outlaws, and neither Calhoun nor Ferris can ride." He turned back up the tracks where Fogarty was. "Damn you, Fogarty."

He was ready to take his anger out on anyone slightly associated with the treasury department. "You people were warned several times about this and you ignored the warnings." He was screaming at Desmond, getting right into his face. "People have died and more may yet. Heads will roll before I'm through with this situation." He sincerely hoped that someone would challenge him. Bull Morrison needed to whip the dickens out of someone or something.

"If I can't get them to a doctor then I've got to get a doctor out here." Morrison looked around for Squash and called him over. "Ride hard back to the station and get help, Squash. If they don't have a doctor bring a wagon back so we can get these people back to Carson City. They're in bad shape."

Desmond got his act together, fearing that Morrison would take all his frustrations out on him. "One of our agents left out on foot to do that, Marshal. Sam Arnold is probably at the station now. The train was only a few miles out from there."

"Did something right, anyway," Morrison said. "Go anyway, Squash. We are going to need a wagon no matter what. Hurry."

SAM ARNOLD WAS IN GOOD SHAPE, but he was dressed in heavy winter clothing and hadn't run for long distances in a long time. He started out at a fast run and knew immediately that was the wrong thing to do. Easing back to a jog, he made considerable distance before he had to stop and catch his breath.

It was well over an hour when he jogged into the watering and fuel station. He was stopped by Station Master Small. "Wreck," Arnold stammered. "Men injured. Help," he said. He collapsed to the muddy ground and Small yelled for two nearby men to get the man inside the station. He was bundled in and laid out on a wooden bench near a pot belly stove.

"Get some water," Small ordered. He got Arnold's coat off and used it as a pillow. "Now, slowly, tell me what this is all about."

"Train blown up and men hurt. Heard shooting. Send help." He was gasping out the words and was also trying to sit up.

Small stood up, looked around and Bull Morrison's warning of an attack came flooding back. "The marshal was right, and Fogarty wasn't ready," he murmured. He called for several of the men to get a team hitched, find the Mound House Doctor, Enid Watson, and be ready to move. "Jason, send a wire to Carson City and to Virginia City. The line is closed until further notice. Make sure Abe Curry at the mint is notified of this."

In the midst of the flurry of activity, Squash Malone rode into the station area at a full gallop, jumped from the horse and ran into the station house. "Where's the station master?" He yelled.

"I'm Stan Small. You're one of the marshals, aren't you? We just got word of the wreck."

"We have wounded, marshals and outlaws. Need a wagon and strong team. Is there a doctor in this area?"

"Team, wagon, and doctor will be ready to move shortly, Marshal. Did everyone survive?"

"I'm afraid not. The engineer was killed in the explosion. It's a hell of a mess up there."

Small had to sit down. "Engineer Peltry, dead? Oh, my.

I'll have to send word to his wife, Annie. Oh, my, those dear children. You said outlaws? They were captured?"

"Yes, two of them, wounded, but in chains."

Squash had his mind set on getting help while Small already had his mind working on clearing the wreckage and getting that busy line reopened. Two railroad men had the wagon and harnessed team ready as Doc Watson walked in. "How many injured?" He asked.

"Four, all bullet wounds," Squash answered. He yelled at Sam Arnold to drive the wagon and helped the doc with his medical supplies into the wagon. "I'll ride ahead." He was back in the saddle and racing down the tracks.

Watson had treated many gunshot wounds during time in the army and along the frontier and urged Arnold on. "Heavy bleeding is what kills so many after being shot, man. Kick those horses up. The quicker you get me there, the better chance they'll live."

STAN FERRIS WAS ON THE GROUND, laid out next to the now conscious Slim Calhoun when Desmond and one other treasury agent brought the unconscious John Ivory over. "Keep him separated from the two of us. When you bring the woman, be careful. She's a killer and will slit your throat without thinking about it." Ferris pointed to an area about ten feet on the other side of Calhoun. "Over there would be good. How are you feeling Slim?"

"Like I was hit by that train. Arm is killing me. You don't look so good yourself."

The bullet in Ferris's hip had burrowed through muscle and bone, ached something fierce, and kept him from sitting up. On his stomach, he watched them lay Ivory out and pulled his gun. "Sure as I'm layin' here all busted up one of 'em is gonna try something stupid." Just moments later Morrison walked up holding Linda Bricky tight.

"Sit down and don't move," Morrison said, shoving her to the ground next to Ivory. Blood was running from numerous cuts and scrapes on her face, her leg wound was bleeding, and one of the treasury agents made a move to help her.

"Back off," Morrison growled. "These are my prisoners. Nobody touches them until the doc gets here." He bent down to Calhoun and pulled a set of hand cuffs from his coat, reached in his coat and found another pair. "You, Desmond, come here. I'm going to hold that wildcat there and you put these on her. You do know how, don't you?" Slim had to chuckle.

"I think I could actually see the sarcasm, Bull. You're getting much better at that."

Desmond mumbled something and took the offered cuffs while Morrison jerked Bricky to her feet. She was in considerable pain and Morrison used that to his advantage. She couldn't kick him because of the wounded leg and couldn't hit or scratch him because Morrison had her arms pinned behind her.

"That hurts. You're a brute," she screamed. She tried to wrench an arm free, to hit the marshal and couldn't. Instead, she tried to bite him, and Morrison whacked her hard across the side of the head, splashing blood on Desmond who was fighting to get the cuffs on the squirming woman. "Damn it, hold still," Desmond said bringing a guffaw from Morrison.

"I didn't say you had to be gentle, Desmond. Get 'em on her," he bellowed. He finally got them locked on with her hands behind her. Morrison shoved Bricky to the ground. "Now, Desmond, sit that fool Ivory up with his back to Bricky, pull his arms behind him and interlock their arms before you put the cuffs on him. Got it?" He made it sound like he was talking to a child, which brought more chuckles from Calhoun and Ferris. Morrison had Bricky by the shoulders, standing over her, ready to smack her again if she gave Desmond more trouble.

"This is gonna be one hell of a ride to Carson City," Sandy Ferris chuckled, slipping his revolver back in the holster.

"I think we'll let Buffalo Butch Endicott ride in the back of the wagon with our prisoners," Morrison laughed.

"You should have seen him, Marshal. He was like an angel working on Calhoun. He hummed some kind of song and was softer than anything I've ever seen. I would not have believed it if I hadn't seen it. He's up where the dead engineer is, working on the fireman now. They call him Gus, the fireman. He got hit with a piece of steel too but didn't say anything until he fell down from weakness."

"Damn," Morrison said. "It didn't have to happen. None of it." He stormed around the little area. "Nobody had to die, nobody had to get shot." He was about to walk off to find Fogarty and have it out with the fool when Squash Malone came racing in.

CHAPTER 17

"WAGON AND DOCTOR COMING, BULL. HOW'S SLIM?"

"Laughin' it off. He'll be fine. You said doctor? More than I expected. Bricky's gonna give us trouble, Squash. Ivory's still out." Morrison looked around and saw Desmond. "You, take one of your people and help Butch Endicott bring the fireman down here with anyone else who might be wounded."

Morrison was watching the fires in the boxcars and realized there was at least one person missing. "Shouldn't there be one more train person? Where's the conductor, the boss of the train?"

"They usually ride in the caboose," Stan Ferris said. "It's layin' on its side back there and looks like it might start burnin' soon, too. Probably a busted lamp."

Morrison and Malone raced down the length of the train, evading or jumping over debris and burning bushes. With the railcar on its side it was hard getting the door at the back of the car open but did get in after some hard work. "There he is," Squash said. He was pointing at a table that was bolted to the floor. The conductor was trapped between the table and the splintered side of the caboose, wedged in.

"Easy now, fella," Morrison said. "We'll get you out of here." A lamp had been flung to the ground by the wreck and flames were moving up the flooring of the car. "I think it's that chair that has him wedged tight. See if you can rip it out of there."

Squash Malone had the chair ripped in pieces before getting it out and away from the bolted table, and Morrison eased the conductor out from under the mess. "Doesn't look like any broken bones, so let's see if you can stand up. What's your name?"

"Patterson," he said. "Dick Patterson." He grabbed Morrison's outreached hand and eased himself to his feet. "Couldn't get myself untangled down there. Head hurts."

"It should," Morrison said. "You took a good blow to the back of your head. Come on, we gotta get out of here. We have help coming."

"What the hell happened?" Patterson was wobbly, and Squash helped get him out of the overturned railcar. "We were picking up speed when all hell broke loose."

"It did that," Morrison laughed. "It did, indeed. Outlaws blew up the engine and tracks, but we got 'em."

"Who's we?" The conductor was able to walk, slowly, and Morrison was leading them back to where the others were.

"I'm U.S. Marshal Bull Morrison. My deputies and I caught the outlaws but not before they blew up the train. The engineer was killed and there are other injuries. A doctor is on the way, so just relax until he gets here."

Sam Arnold drove the wagon into the wreck area and Butch Endicott directed him to where the injured were. Doctor Watson jumped down with his kit bag. "Bring those sheets and blankets and I'll want as much hot water as you can get." He walked up to where everyone was laid out.

"I thought you said four people with bullet wounds? Someone can't count very well." Watson counted six wounded and injured people and started checking them one at a time.

"Those two there are dangerous outlaws, Doc. They be looked at last, and only when a deputy marshal is at your side." Morrison nodded to Ivory and Bricky. "Those two there are deputy marshals and need to be treated as fast as possible. The others are train personnel."

"You have your thoughts Marshal and I have my ways," Watson said. Desmond and treasury agent Zeb Watkins brought large pans of hot water from the wrecked engine while Conductor Patterson and Butch Endicott ripped up sheets for bandages, and Doc Watson got started.

"The conductor and fireman have head injuries, Doc," Endicott said. "I have the fireman's head cleaned and wrapped, but they just brought out the conductor." He went on to describe the wounds to Calhoun and Ferris.

"You've done a good job," Doc Watson said. "Stick with me and be my extra hands."

"CAN YOU HEAR ME?" Linda Bricky was whispering over her shoulder to Ivory. They were sitting back to back, their arms intertwined and cuffed. "John T. Can you hear me?"

"Yeah," he whispered. "Hurt bad, Linda. Can't breathe."

"I might be able to get my hands out of these cuffs. Can you?" She was angry again because of his crying about being hurt. *To think I gave myself to that fool. I'm gonna get away and ain't never giving myself to another man-child.*

"They're on tight. I'm too weak to get loose. Lost too much blood." His voice was as weak as his body and Linda wanted to laugh right out at him. "This might be the end for us," he said.

"Not for me," she said. She was seeing a vague but possible plan. *If she could get that one that locked her cuffs on to get interested in her, she might be able to get away. If I can get his gun I can get away.* She was watching all the activity around the wounded men, slowly working one hand free of the cuffs without drawing attention. It was harder than she thought but could feel that she was making progress.

Doctor Watson was moving from man to man making his assessments of their wounds before starting treatment since considerable aid had already been given. "You did a fine job on these wounds."

"Thank you. It's been a gift, I have. I can almost feel the pain myself when I find a hurt or injured animal or person."

"You would have made a fine doctor. A large one, but a fine one," Watson said.

"Let's take a look at that arm, Marshal Calhoun." Watson had Calhoun's jacket and shirt ripped away and was cleaning the open wound. "Bone's broke below the elbow and there's considerable damage to the muscle, but you'll be fine in a few weeks. Got some sewing to do here, and it's gonna hurt." Doc Watson turned to Desmond. "Find Endicott for me. I need his size and strength." He went back to Calhoun's wound.

"Grit your teeth a bit, son. This will hurt," and he set the bones in place to Calhoun's howl of pain. "There, that'll hold. Didn't hurt too much, now, did it." He chuckled and got some nasty words back. He patched the wound and got splints in place as Butch Endicott settled down next to him.

"Wanted something, Doc?"

"Yup." Doc Watson was amazed by the size of the man who settled in next to him. "Hold that arm in place. Don't let the splints move, and I'll wrap this up." Watson watched the huge man's mighty fingers hold the splints and steady the arm as if he had worked with a physician daily. "Good job. Thank you. Were you in the war? You seem to have done this before."

"No, not the war. I've worked in stone quarries for years and the injuries can be far more nasty than these. I know pain, Doc."

"As I," Doc Watson said. He gathered his kit and moved to Sandy Ferris. "This next man was shot in the hip, so it might be a little awkward to patch him," he chuckled.

"Get yourself a cup of hot coffee, Slim," Endicott said.

"You'll be on your feet in no time. Bull's bringing the pot down now." Endicott had Slim's arm in a sling and gave him a solid whack on his good shoulder. "Coming, Doc."

Linda Bricky was watching the doctor and motioned for Desmond to come over. "Did someone mention coffee?" Her eyes were on the man, appraising, if you will. She gave the treasury agent a big smile, then winced as if in pain, and slumped back. "Sure could use some coffee."

"They're bringing some down, Miss. Are you in bad pain?"

"My leg really hurts," she cried, softly. Suck all this in you idiot. I want you to be my best friend coz my hands are almost loose. Another thought entered her mind. Maybe I can get him to unlock the cuffs so I can drink the coffee. "I sure hope the doc can make my leg feel better."

Desmond stood and looked around for Bull Morrison and the coffee and walked to where he had a fire going and the pot boiling. "That lady's leg is hurting real bad, Marshal and she wonders if she could have a cup of that coffee?"

"I told you to stay away from the prisoners and I meant it. Go near them again and you'll be one." Morrison snarled it out, almost jumping to his feet. "Were you fool enough to ask her how she planned to drink that coffee? Have you ever been within five hundred feet of a dangerous prisoner? Damn. Your badge said deputy. Deputy behind a desk all day every day?"

Desmond stepped back quickly and was unable to say anything. No one had ever talked to him this way. But, he thought, the man's right. I've never been anywhere near a criminal. I've always been at a desk. He realized, too, that Fogarty had never been in the field before, either.

Morrison poured himself a tin cup of hot coffee. "Follow me," he said and walked over to Bricky. Desmond was half a step behind him. "Here you go, Sweetie," he said. He held the cup out for her. "Come on, now. You asked for coffee? Here it is," he teased.

"Bastard," she howled. That was followed by a string of nasty words and comments that had Doctor Watson almost red with embarrassment.

"Shame on you," he said. "That is no way for a young lady to behave."

"She ain't no lady, Doc, believe me," Slim Calhoun said. "That man she's chained up to ain't no gentleman, either."

Morrison laughed softly as he drank the coffee. "She's wanted for murder and bank robbery, Agent Desmond. We don't cater to murderers in the marshal service. Don't make me say any of this again." Morrison walked to the fire and got another cup for his deputy.

"Gonna be a wild ride back to Carson City, Slim. You gonna be ready for that?"

"Between Buffalo Butch Endicott and Doctor Watson, I'm gonna be fine, Bull. A little weak right now, but a few more cups of your mud and I'll be fine. We need to get all the stuff from our camp down here. Food, Bull, there's food in that camp."

"I sent Squash out to pick it all up. The pack animals can carry it all. He'll be back soon. I think our best bet is to stay right here tonight and then pack up and move out at first light. Give the wounded a good night's sleep after some hot food."

"Good idea. We'll need to keep close watch on Ivory and Bricky. She's slick as hell, Bull, and these treasury people aren't field agents. They spend their time behind desks, don't even know not to approach prisoners."

"I don't know which one I'll shoot first, Desmond or Fogarty," Morrison laughed. "Will you be able to move about soon? Gonna be a long night."

"I can move. When do you suppose our first visitors will arrive? Sure as hell the word of the wreck is out by now."

CHAPTER 18

"Do you really think it's best to spend the night out here, Marshal? These wounded and injured people can sleep in warm beds at my little facility at Mound House." Doctor Watson had done a splendid job getting everyone patched and splinted but had never been in contact with vicious killers before. With Morrison hovering over him every second, Watson was able to work on Bricky's leg and face but needed more room to work on Ivory.

"We have to get him separated from her, Marshal. The man's in critical condition, has lost too much blood, and might die soon if I can't get to the wound."

"I understand your concern for the wounded, Doc. You must understand my concern that some of the wounded outlaws are capable or hurting or killing those that might get too close. Some of these people are on the way to the gallows and are desperate."

"Yes, yes, of course," Doc Watson said. "I do understand that, but this man is dying."

It was a fight of wills, but Bull Morrison finally let compassion rule and unlocked Ivory from Bricky. "Lock her arms around something strong and behind her back," he told Squash. "Kick her in the head if she fights you." Morrison wasn't kidding.

Squash moved her over to where the wagon was and sat her down with her back to one of the huge rear wheels. "She ain't moving the wagon, Bull, but might bend it a bit." He laughed, coming back from the ordeal. "She's a wildcat."

"That's all of them, then." Morrison turned back to Doc Watson to discuss why he wanted to spend the night at the wreck scene. "With hot fires and hot food, we'll be fine right here for tonight, Doc. Those two outlaws are already figuring out how to escape, and I ain't gonna let 'em." Morrison was okay with Doctor Watson not being wise to the ways of outlaws but was worried about Fogarty's less than professional agents. "Moving 'em tonight would give them one more chance at breaking free and staying will give my deputies a good night's sleep to get well. I'll need every one of them on the trip to Carson City."

"Been a long time since I slept on the ground, Marshal, but I do know how. I'll change everyone's dressings in the morning before you pull out. Young Sandy Ferris will have to ride in the wagon. That hip wound will keep him off his feet and out of the saddle for at least three weeks. Deputy Calhoun will be able to ride with little difficulty."

"How about the train men? I really don't want them to have to ride in the wagon with the prisoners. Too dangerous."

"The fireman can ride. He took a chunk of steel to his back and another to the head but neither wound is critical. He'll be fine, just sore. The conductor took a nasty smack to the back of his head. He has no balance, loss of memory, and is in pain. He'll have to ride in the wagon."

"Thank you, Doc. I assume the train men will be staying at your clinic in Mound House? Won't be riding all the way into Carson City?" Morrison enjoyed the nod back from Watson. It meant these would be people he wouldn't be responsible for.

The big marshal walked over to where Calhoun was sitting next to Ferris and Endicott. "I don't suppose anyone has a bottle?" He said.

Morrison was aware that wires had been sent out about the attempted robbery and was surprised that the Carson City Sheriff hadn't come out. Also, it surprised him that Fogarty hadn't set guards around the shipment, even if some of it was gnarled and melted. It was still gold and silver. He saw the agent sitting off by himself and walked over.

"We're bound to have visitors before long, Fogarty. Wires were sent out about the attack on the shipment and hordes of looky-looks will be arriving. How are you planning to guard that gold this time?"

"I have Sam Arnold and Zeb Watkins down at the wrecked express car, Marshal. I'm sure Abe Curry has people on the way to collect and return the gold."

"You're the most arrogant and foolish person I've ever met," Morrison said. "What kind of relationship do you have with the Ormsby County Sheriff? When word gets out that this train is on its side, that there are thousands of dollars in slightly melted gold coins on the ground, every snot of an outlaw will be swarming this wreck."

Fogarty just looked at him. It had never entered his mind that people living in and around the area might descend on the wreck and steal the coins. Never thought about creating a relationship with the local sheriff in Carson City. In Washington, D.C., the idea of coming west for this project was the opportunity of a lifetime. The fact that responsibility came with the trip wasn't factored in.

What Fogarty had in his limited vision was being able to talk about visiting the fabulous Virginia City, seeing gold and silver ripped from the ground and become coins of the realm at a mint he was involved in. After all, cocktail parties in the nation's capitol were host to many beautiful women who would delight in his stories.

"You do not deserve the badge you wear." Morrison had to turn and walk away before he let his anger run wild. He went back to the fire and called Squash Monroe and Slim Calhoun over. "Squash go get all our people and bring them here. One more big problem, I'm afraid." Squash had Butch Endicott and the train people over quickly. "Grab some coffee coz we got another problem."

The big marshal spoke quickly. "We'll surely have locals and others swarming the area soon. You train men are badly wounded, so stay near the fire. Slim, you, Butch, and Squash will have to guard the gold. We won't get much help from the treasury people."

He looked back and forth at those sitting around the fire and was surprised to find that most were wounded. "First off, I'm somewhat amazed the sheriff isn't here. Two, I'm surprised that we haven't already had unwelcome visitors. Three, what the hell do we do about it?"

"With Fogarty completely out of his element, with two wounded prisoners, and with gold and silver just lying about, all over the ground, all hell is about to happen." Morrison reached across and grabbed a bottle of brandy that had been in their packs, and took a long drink, offering the bottle to Slim, as if to say, give me an answer that will work.

Too many times, Slim thought, he and Bull Morrison had been in this kind of predicament. There were always wounded prisoners and never enough people. "Just not enough of us, Bull. The longer these prisoners are not behind bars the more opportunity they'll have to try something. The longer that gold and silver sits out there without strong protection, the more apt it will be stolen."

Calhoun looked to Sandy Ferris and he had to crawl a little closer to the fire. "Couldn't get shot in the leg or arm, oh hell no, not me. I had to take one in the hip." Squash couldn't hold back his snicker. "It isn't funny," Ferris snapped. He took the offered bottle and drank deep. "You working on a plan, Marshal?"

"We are," Morrison said. "When the word of this attempted robbery reached Carson City how do you think that sheriff of yours would react? Would he send people out here? We could sure use some serious help about now."

"You wouldn't get it from him, I'm afraid. If any of his deputies arrive, watch 'em close, Marshal. They'll have that gold in their pokes in seconds." Ferris eased his painful body closer to the fire and took another swig of the good stuff before handing it off. "Sam Pasternak is an outlaw himself, Marshal. Don't look for help there."

"I'm not sure what kind of help you're looking for, Marshal," Conductor Dick Patterson said. "The fireman and I have pretty serious head wounds, but we'll try to do anything you ask. I'm sure Stan Small will have railroad people up here first thing in the morning. We can't let this main line to the Comstock stay closed."

"I might have to call on you, Dick, but we'll try to keep you out of harm's way. If we can," he snorted.

"You're gonna have to pull Fogarty's people in, Bull." Slim Calhoun waited for the explosion, but surprisingly, it didn't come. "They're badge carrying treasury agents, Bull. They'll do what they're told by the person in charge. What they don't have in Fogarty is that strong person in charge."

"I hope you're right," Morrison said. "Squash, gather them up, including Fogarty, and bring them here. Mr. Patterson, will you be kind enough to take a shotgun and sit with our prisoners? Don't get close, don't talk to them, and shoot them dead if they try something stupid." He looked around at his squad and forced a horrible smile, grabbing the bottle from Slim Calhoun.

"MY GOD, THIS IS HORRIBLE." Abe Curry said when the telegram from Mound House arrived. "They blew up the train, killed the engineer, but the outlaws have been captured. Amazing." Curry called in one of his assistants and had him copy the wire and get it over to the sheriff as fast as possible. "Pasternak has to respond to this. That shipment must be protected." The man hurried off and Curry sank deep into his rather plush chair in the mint's office. The very first shipment from this elegant structure, robbed? Oh, my God. Those men from Washington were warned more than once and ignored the word of a U.S. Marshal. He had a worried look on his face, dejected even, and knew he was too far from the action to even think of doing something.

Curry couldn't think of anything that he could do, he didn't have people to recover that gold and silver, now scattered about in the great Nevada desert. "When word of this gets out, every down and out fool is going to race for that wreck." He was talking to himself, got up and headed out the door.

"She's just a saloon owner but Irene Thorndyke was very close to those marshals. She might have some kind of answer." It took less than five minutes to thread his way from the mint to the Palace Club, and he settled in at the end of the bar, right next to Henry Honeycutt.

"The train was blown up, Henry." Curry motioned for Irene to come join them, and waited for her to settle in. "Outlaws are in custody, but that shipment is spread all over the ground out there, waiting to be picked up. Is there anything at all that we can do?"

"Pasternak will send his men to pilfer, Abe," Irene said. "No help there. Slim and Bull will need men with guns, men with integrity not empty pockets."

"Of course," Abe Curry said. "My own guards. Why didn't I think of that. Henry, can you bring them here? It will be easier to make plans if we can use some of your tables in the back, Irene."

Henry Honeycutt limped his way across North Carson Street while Irene and Curry set up tables in the back of the saloon. She motioned the barman, Leroy, to bring a couple of pitchers of beer and a few steins to the table. Curry frowned but didn't say anything.

"I doubt if any of those men have riding horses, Abe. Maybe a few with buggies, but they'll need to ride out to the wreck." Irene paced about, trying to figure out where she might find six horses.

"No, Irene, I'll send them out in a big wagon with four-up. They'll need to bring the shipment back, remember." She wondered why she didn't think of that.

"I'll leave you and Henry to get the men started on that chore, and I'll take care of the bar," She said. It was just minutes and Henry was back with the six burly teamsters who had been acting as site guards. Each carried a shotgun, a couple had rifles, and all had sidearms strapped in place. Abe Curry outlined the problem and conjured up the plans as the men drank a glass of beer or two.

"I'm putting a big load on you men, I know," Curry said. "But you've done such a fine job protecting the construction site, I know you'll work well with the marshals. Monaghan, you're still the lead man, and I'll expect you to follow the orders as laid out by Marshal Morrison."

"Aye, Abe," Michael Fitzgerald Monaghan laughed. "Morrison whipped old Endicott; I'll surely do as he says." Generous laughter flowed around the table. Six men all had the same thoughts, bring that gold back to Carson City.

"We'll need two of those freight wagons, Abe. That load all but filled the express car and many of those crates must be broken."

Abe Curry agreed and the meeting broke up. Curry led the six men to the mint carriage house to harness the teams and head for Mound House. It was rapidly getting dark as they drove out of Carson City.

CHAPTER 19

Morrison had the main campfire blazing, making Slim Calhoun laugh right out. "Good thing we're not in hostile Indian country, Bull. Probably be able to see those flames in Salt Lake City." The marshal used broken timbers from wrecked boxcars, tore out great stands of sage, and enjoyed every minute of it. Slim Calhoun was always amazed watching Bull Morrison around a campfire. The man was obsessed with them, and the bigger the fire, the better.

"I expect to see you with a drum dancing frantically about, some day."

"Ain't no reason for a dinky little fire on a cold night like is coming on, Slim, and don't you forget it." He was surrounded by everyone except Squash Malone, Doctor Watson, and the prisoners. "Settle in everyone, coz I'm not gonna be repeating what I'm about to say. Doc Watson is guarding the prisoners and Squash Malone is guarding the gold while we talk, so you better listen good."

Bull Morrison had been a leader almost from childhood. Men followed him because he led, he didn't follow, never asked anyone to do something he couldn't do, and Slim Calhoun often had to remind him that there were others to help get the job done. Slim looked around the campfire and saw that Morrison had, indeed, everyone's attention.

"For the record, I'm Senior U.S. Marshal Bull Morrison and as of this moment I'm in charge. All of you will do as I say, no questions asked. If you don't you will be placed under arrest and will find yourselves in irons along with our notorious outlaws." He paused for a breath, glared at the treasury agents and continued. "Some of you work for the treasury department, but right now, you work for me. Some of you work for the railroad, but right now, you work for me." He walked to the coffee pot and poured half a tin cup full, filling the rest with brandy.

"The word has spread across the western states that an attack on this shipment has been made, that the train was wrecked, and that the railcar holding the shipment was blown up. We will be having scores of visitors at any moment and it is our job to protect the shipment as best we can, and to not let the prisoners escape. Each of you will be assigned to work with one of the marshals and you will do as you're told. Questions?"

Slim Calhoun couldn't hold back the smile that spread across his rugged face. This was Bull Morrison at his best. Big, strong, assertive, and intimidating. Men would follow this man, cowards would shrink from him, and the weak would gain strength from him. "Think we might get help, Bull?" He asked.

"If you're thinking the sheriff in Carson City, no. From Abe Curry at the mint? Maybe."

"I'll detail the treasury agents," Fogarty said, standing up and moving toward the coffee pot.

"No, you won't," Morrison boomed. "I'll detail you and everyone else here. If you choose to fight me on this, Fogarty, I'll place you under arrest and you know damn well I have that authority. This is my crime scene. I'm in charge and that's the final word. Fight me and it'll be your last fight."

It was Butch Endicott who broke things up with a howl of laughter. "Ah, Mr. Fogarty, let me tell you how that fight might end."

The only sound was that of genuine laughter from the marshals, and the crackling of the large fire. Treasury agents looked back and forth between Bull Morrison and Thaddeus Winston Fogarty and saw immediately that Fogarty had folded his cards. He sat by the fire, looking down at the ground, shaking in his anger, but unwilling to challenge a U.S. Marshal.

Morrison took the silence as acceptance and continued. "Here's how I want us to work as the night goes on. I think the real trouble will come at or about sunrise." He pulled a folded sheet of paper from his coat pocket and started reading names, making assignments.

MIKE MONAGHAN DROVE the horses hard and made good time through the Carson River Canyon and up to the railhead at Mound House. Traffic was heaviest during the daylight hours and there was little in the evenings. The five brawny teamsters had two large freight wagons to protect and haul the gold and silver coins back to Carson City. It was getting late and the temperature was falling fast.

"What's the word from the wreck site?" He asked Stan Small without climbing down from his high seat on his freight wagon. "Mr. Curry's afraid people will swarm the site and rob the shipment clean, he is."

"So is that Marshal Morrison," Small said. "They'll be glad to see you, Michael. I'm putting together the crew to clear the site and rebuild the tracks. Those trains gotta move."

Monaghan howled at the sweat speckled horses and moved out at a solid trot for the final ride to the wreck. "Sounds like we got here in time boys." It was fully dark, but they had no trouble following the tracks. They were some ways off when they saw the flames from Bull's campfire.

"Gonna be warm, anyway," one of the teamsters laughed. Monaghan led the wagons to the fire and was challenged immediately by shotgun toting Slim Calhoun.

"Come one more yard and die," Calhoun yelled out. "Stop now," he ordered. Monaghan pulled the teams up and hollered back.

"We're from the mint. Sent by Mr. Curry. I'm Monaghan," he yelled.

"Glad you're here. Take care of your wagons and horses and join us at the fire." Calhoun stepped out from behind the tree he used for a shield and waved at the group before turning back to the fire. "Curry sent his site guards and two wagons, Bull. Looks to be about five or six of them. We've got the backup we've been hoping for."

"Glory be," Morrison said. "That changes things in our favor. I want you and Squash to take charge of protecting that shipment. Take one or two of the treasury people. That will give you ten guns and should be plenty. Of course, the rest of us will be available at your call." Morrison threw more wood on the already blazing fire and took a healthy swipe of brandy.

"The two train men are hurting bad, Ivory may not make the night according to Doc Watson, and I'll keep everyone else busy around here. I want to pull out just as soon as possible." Morrison was pacing back and forth, obviously worried about something.

"We can't just ride off, though," Slim Calhoun said. "We can't leave until that pile of gold and silver is in the wagons."

"I know, I know," Morrison said. He watched the six teamsters come back from taking care of the horses and wagons and motioned for them to get comfortable by the fire. "Most of you know me by now," he said. "I'm U.S. Marshal Bull Morrison and this is my Deputy, Slim Calhoun. I'm going to ask a lot of you men but please understand we have a huge problem here.

Along with many thousands of dollars in gold and silver scattered about, we have two killers in irons, and several seriously wounded people." His pacing had slowed, and Calhoun recognized that Morrison had decided on a plan. "How long would it take you to load those wagons with the gold if you didn't have to worry about being attacked?"

Monaghan looked around at his crew and back to Morrison and Calhoun. "About a solid six hours, Marshal. We'd have it loaded by sunrise if we didn't have to also stand guard."

"That's what I wanted to hear," Morrison said. Slim could see the worry wash off the big man. There was even the slightest hint of that horrible attempt at smiling. "That's what I want you to do, but keep those rifles and shotguns close at hand." He ripped another sage from the ground and heaped in on the fire.

"It's gonna be a miserable night, I'm afraid. Slim, you and Squash stand guard while Monaghan and his boys load that wagon, Take two of the treasury agents with you." He took a long drink of brandy. "Leave Fogarty here with me. The rest of us will see to it that the camp, wounded, and prisoners are ready to pull out at first light. Let's move."

A DEPUTY ALMOST RAN into Sam Pasternak's office with the wire from Abe Curry. "The mint shipment was attacked, Sheriff." Pasternak was a mean man in looks and action, tall and thin, with receding dark hair, brown eyes, long thin nose that had been broken at least twice, and a grim look to his mouth. His thin lips rarely smiled unless the conversations were about money that could be his. Like the wrecking of a train load of gold.

"Isn't that a shame," Pasternak said. He took the offered wire and read it. "Better put together a posse, Thomas. Only our people. No townspeople." His eyes had narrowed, his thin lips offered the hint of an evil grin, and he leaned back in his swivel chair. "Sure hope nothing horrible happened to those federal people," he snickered.

Ian Thomas gave a knowing nod and smile and walked out of the office. Sam Pasternak leaned back, lit a cheroot, and read the note again. "So the rumors were true," he mumbled. He was already working on how to get as much of that gold into his pockets as possible, knowing too, that he had to return at least some of it to the mint. He walked out of the office and into the large outer room, now filled with six deputies, also thinking about how much gold would fill their pockets.

I'd like to take the boys at Warm Springs but I don't dare. This has to look like it's a sheriff's office mission and those boys aren't deputies. Pasternak owned the Warm Springs saloons and whore houses and had a gang of men living there. Stage robberies, bank jobs, and strong-arm robberies were their specialties and Pasternak protected them at all costs.

"We'll let Abe Curry worry about getting the gold back to Carson City, boys. We'll protect what we can," he said with a sly and well-practiced smile. The men understood that to mean what they could jam in their pockets and still keep their pants up. "There are federal agents up there, but they are the ones that we've met at the mint. Don't pay any attention to them and don't take any guff either."

"What about the rumor of federal marshals being in town, Sam? Think it's true?" Ian Thomas was Pasternak's chief deputy, wanted in Texas and Arizona Territory for murder and bank robbery. "Might mean trouble."

"For them," Pasternak laughed. "Treat 'em the same as the treasury jerks." He chuckled and walked to the door. "We'll ride out after midnight. I'd like to be able to ride into the wreck site as the day gets light. Probably a ten-mile ride."

Pasternak walked into the sheriff's corral area and the barn where all the tack and feed were stored. Instead of leather saddle bags he attached large canvas bags to the back of his saddle. "They'll hold a considerable amount, I do believe."

The seven-man posse was assembled and rode out of town about two in the morning, unaware of Curry's six-man recovery unit or the number of men Morrison had. Every man riding for Sam Pasternak had only gold on his mind as they rode at a brisk trot toward the Carson River Canyon. It was near four in the morning when they passed through the Mound House switching yard, following the rail line north to the wreck. A practiced eye might see a slight lightening of the eastern sky.

"We're gonna want to assert our authority, Ian." Pasternak had the men riding at a strong trot through the bitter cold morning. "We'll ride right into whatever kind of camp they might have, and I'll take charge of whatever they have going. Follow my lead and don't shoot until either they do or I do."

CHAPTER 20

WITH FIRES BURNING BRIGHT, THE JOB OF LOADING THE MINT SHIPMENT into the freight wagons was fast and orderly. "We're bound to miss some of the coins from broken cases, but we can get them when the sun comes up," Mike Monaghan said. He and Slim Calhoun were standing near the wrecked express car.

"Or the railroad workers when they come to fix this mess." Monaghan knew that would be their first effort after arriving. "Looks like most of the shipment survived."

"I thought there would be a lot more damage," Slim said. "That was one hell of an explosion and fire."

"These crates are solid, Marshal. They'll take a good whacking before coming apart. You're putting a lot of pressure on that arm of yours, Marshal. Don't make that wound any worse for the wear. Was that mean looking marshal serious worrying if the sheriff showed up?"

"From everything we've heard, Pasternak is more outlaw than sheriff. Let's get this wrapped up, Mike. It's gettin' light fast."

"Hope that old freight wagon holds together," Monaghan chuckled. "Come on boys, tie everything down tight and make ready for the road. Somebody wake Porterfield, he's driving number two. I'll take the lead."

The teamsters let one man sleep the night away. Morrison had most of his people get some sleep too. "That's a long road into Carson City, and even though it's a busy road, with all that gold we will be a target."

Morrison never let the fire die down and was standing near it when he heard riders coming on fast. He howled out a warning and scrambled for his weapon of choice, a double-barreled ten-gauge shotgun loaded with buckshot. Ferris, even though he couldn't do anything but lay on his stomach, had a rifle in hand, as did those coming out of their bedrolls.

Calhoun spread the mint guards around the wagons, and he and Squash Malone took up positions in the wrecked railcar. "Sounds like half a dozen or more," Slim said. "Don't shoot until I do. Let's not start a war unless we have to."

Pasternak led his posse right into the camp but didn't step off his horse. "I'm Sheriff Pasternak," he shouted. "Where are the shipment guards? We're here to take the shipment back to Carson City."

"Afraid not, Sheriff." Bull Morrison stepped out from a broken and half burned pine tree, the shotgun comfortably cradled, cocked, and almost aimed at the eight riders. "I'm U.S. Marshal Bull Morrison. The mint shipment is under my care. Appreciate you riding out like this. You can help escort us and our prisoners back to Carson City."

"To hell with that," Deputy Ian Thomas yelled out. He jerked his rifle up and took a load of buckshot to his mid-section, blowing him ten feet back and onto the ground, dead. Pasternak and the rest of his posse sank spurs and raced to the open sagebrush, firing their weapons wildly as they ran. They rode over a rise in the prairie and jumped from their saddles when they were clear.

"Damn fool," Pasternak growled. "He shouldn't have made

that play, boys. We gotta finish this now. They gotta die. They know who we are."

There was scattered gunfire from Morrison's side and Morrison yelled for it to stop. "Let's shoot at known targets, not the cold morning air," he howled.

"Stay with the wagon," Calhoun yelled at Monaghan. "Keep your people ready to move, Mike. Desmond, you and Arnold stay too." He wanted to say more to the treasury agents but didn't. He wanted to say, 'this was your job in the first place.' Wanted to say, 'Should have had your horses on that train,' but held off. His wound ached from the hard work loading all the gold but the rest of him was ready for a fight.

He and Squash ran to a line of burnt trees between the express wagon and the main camp site. "See where they went?"

"Out about fifty yards or so. There's a small rise and deep swale behind it. Deep enough to hide their horses. Let's use the campfire to our advantage, Slim."

"You mean, stay as far away from it as we can." They laughed and moved at a low crouch toward the rise in the prairie. "Anything that moves in front of us is them, Squash. Shoot first and ask questions later."

"Yup," Squash Malone said. "You keep going straight at 'em. I'm gonna circle out to the left some."

Calhoun was on his belly moving from sagebrush to cedar bush to rock pile, not seeing or hearing anything. "Hope this doesn't mean they hightailed it," he murmured. "Just getting in gear for a good fight." He neared the rise in the ground, covered in sage and grasses, and hoped that someone would show their head.

Squash moved fast off to the side, staying low. This was his kind of fight, taught to him by his father so many years ago. He was well off to the north and began moving back toward where the sheriff had led his men when he saw them. "Ah, Sheriff, that's not how you set a good defense." He had his rifle cradled as he slowly crawled closer. He picked his man and took a long slow aim at the middle of the man's chest when a shot rang out and he lost his chance. His target crumbled to the ground.

Squash Malone saw his man, on his belly and up along the top of the rise, slump, dead. "Well, I didn't get mine, but somebody got him." He watched as the sheriff yelled for the posse to mount up and ride out. "They'll regroup and attack us again. That man ain't giving up on all this gold."

Squash was on a knee and fired off two quick shots at the running posse. "Too far out," he mumbled. "Hope Bull wants us to chase 'em."

Morrison yelled at Ferris to try and keep track of where the sheriff went and raced to where Ivory and Bricky were mana-cled and found Doc Watson huddled under a sagebrush. "Stay down low, Doc. Where's Fogarty and the other agent?"

"They ran toward where the gold shipment is, Marshal. Just ran off." He was shaking his head as he kept low in the brush. "Don't be worrying about me. I can shoot better than most men, Marshal. I rode with Grant before I became a doctor."

"I knew I liked you," Morrison said. "Keep those two somewhat safe and I'm gonna get me an outlaw sheriff." He snake-crawled through the brush toward where the ground rose, yelling for Ferris not to shoot him.

"I'll do my best," Ferris whispered. He lost sight of the mar-shal immediately and found, too, that he would be looking almost directly at the sun in just moments. The sun would be at the sheriff's back and the posse would have the advantage.

Bull Morrison had made a good ten yards or more when

he spotted a head slowly inching above the rise. "That's a long shot. Old Slim'd tell me not to take it, use the rifle. Ha," he whispered. He pulled his revolver and took a long slow aim squeezing a round off and watching the head and hat disappear with a muted scream. "That's one for me, Slim," he howled out. He was about to start moving forward when he heard horses running. "They're running."

Morrison jumped up and ran to the rise in time to see the sheriff lead his posse off across the broad plain. "He won't go far. I'll put a cartwheel on that." He was joined in a minute or so by Slim Calhoun and Squash Malone. "There's a dead one over there," Morrison said.

"I saw you take him out, Bull. Cost me my shot," Malone said.

"Ain't dead, Bull." Calhoun knelt down next to wounded deputy. "You blew his ear halfway across the state, took a lot of hide with it, but this one will live to hang." The deputy was unconscious, and Calhoun and Morrison dragged him back to where Ivory and Bricky were.

"Got another one for you, Doc," Morrison said. "Can you work on him while we are on the move? We need to get on the road fast. Slim, get down there and get that freight wagon ready to roll."

"It won't be easy, but yes. Mr. Ivory might not make the journey, Marshal. I'll do my best." He shook his head looking at the mangled side of the wounded man's head. "One inch to the left, and he'd be dead. Marshal, you better adjust your sights."

Morrison had to laugh as he walked back to the fire. Adjust my sights. I like you, Doc. Damn, I gotta remember to tell Slim what he said. That fool Pasternak isn't gonna let this gold get away from him. It's all conveniently loaded in those wagons, ready for the taking. He'll just roll it somewhere and hide most of it, then claim he found the rest. It also means that everyone has to die. He doesn't dare leave a witness.

PASTERNAK HELD UP THE POSSE after they were well away from the tracks. "Ain't lettin' that get away from us, boys. Soon as they get moving, we'll ride down on them, hard. Make sure you're loaded, boys. Separate those big wagons from the small one and those on horseback first, then wipe out everyone. No witnesses. Only way this will work. Word gets out it was us and our splendid little lives are over."

What am I going to do with Carlson? That fool will tell the world what we've done. He has to die right along with those mint guards. Should never have brought him along with us. Sheriff Pasternak had doubts about others with him as well and knew he would have to make them disappear soon. Maybe I should have brought Kerrigan and the Warm Springs boys.

Down below, Slim Calhoun was getting the group put together for the five-mile ride back to Mound House. Bull Morrison had Fogarty and two of his deputies off to the side. "We got lucky, Fogarty. Pasternak wasn't expecting resistance, but even so, you ran from what was assigned to you. You and Desmond were told to defend those wounded prisoners. Instead, you ran away from the fight.

"I plan to have you relieved as soon as we get this shipment and those prisoners safely back to Carson City. You don't deserve to wear that badge."

"My job is to protect that shipment, Marshal. That's what I was doing."

"I'm running this show, Fogarty, and your job was protecting those prisoners. I had many people protecting the gold. I need you to get your stupid head into this fight. We're going to get hit again, soon, and I will shoot you if you run off from the fight. Got it?"

Morrison couldn't shake off the anger and stormed around the lineup of wagons and riders, finally finding his horse and jumping into the saddle. "Are we ready, Slim? Does everyone know we're riding into an attack?" Calhoun yelled his answer, ready, back at Morrison. "Good. Check your weapons one more time and let's move out. Holler loud and long if you see or hear something."

Bull Morrison led the caravan out from the wreck site. Morrison rode in front, the buggy with all the wounded followed. There was a driver, one of the treasury agents, and two men with shotguns, one next to the driver, one in the back of the open buggy.

Slim Calhoun and Squash Malone rode behind the buggy and in front of the freight wagons, which were surrounded by the rest of the treasury agents. The mint guards were riding inside the freight wagons with the gold.

"They'll hit us well before we get to Mound House," Squash said. "Where the grade levels off, about a mile in front of us, is where I'd hit."

"That was a major failure on their part, back there. Pasternak is gonna be in a rage. He knows we all have to die, and he told us who he was. He can't let us get back and report what happened." Slim Calhoun could feel a bloody morning developing and saw a flaw in their current situation. There was nobody on the other side of the tracks.

"I gotta talk to Bull." He rode up to the head of the long line of riders and wagons.

"We gotta make a couple of changes, Bull. Gotta get the buggy and wagons much closer together. Gotta get riders out to the sides, all the way around the two big wagons. Pasternak is after the gold but he knows everyone of us has to die. He can't leave a witness." He was using his arms as well, showing how all the defense was on just the trail side of the tracks.

Morrison didn't hesitate and called the caravan to a halt, giving the new orders quickly. He had them moving again in just minutes. "When they come it will be fast and hard," he yelled out. "Don't hesitate half a second. See someone, shoot 'em." He and Slim led, and there were outriders along both sides and at the rear this time. "Good thinking, Slim. That's why you ride with me." Morrison almost got a smile out that time.

"I'm just glad Abe Curry sent those site guards and the big wagons. Sure can't depend on the Washington group. Why did the treasury department send people from Washington? They have agents out here."

"Probably didn't even ask San Francisco or Denver about it," Bull said. "Keep an eye on that Fogarty. He's just as dumb as he is self-centered."

It was broad daylight as they moved toward Mound House. The cold February wind was coming from the southwest, straight in their faces. Calhoun could see clouds building to the west and north and hoped they wouldn't be bringing another storm for at least another day or two.

CHAPTER 21

"Remember, boys. No witnesses." Pasternak had his posse lined up on either side of the tracks and could see dust from the advancing caravan. "Move out now, well off from the tracks, and at my signal, we'll ride 'em down." The sheriff had just five men left after the death of Thomas and the loss of the other deputy. He hoped that would be more than enough. He was not aware that Curry had sent his site guards to the wreck.

The dust soon became wagons and men on horses, but still a long way off. Pasternak wanted this to be a solid, quick raid. Ride hard and shoot anything that moves. He knew Fogarty had four or five men with him but discounted them as office type agents who didn't know how to fight and thought there were only two marshals along for the ride.

With the mint guards inside the freight wagon, Pasternak wasn't able to see them. "Boys, shoot and kill those that are mounted first, then take the wagons. Those big freight wagons must be carrying the gold."

The caravan came to the slight turn in the rails and began the long descent to the Mound House switching yards. Pasternak held his pistol high in the air, fired it once and gave a long howl, like a wounded wolf. The six men, three on each side of the rails, came at a full gallop, pistols barking, rifles ablaze, directly at the sides of the caravan.

The mounted force with Morrison charged immediately and routed the sheriff's posse. Morrison, Calhoun, and Squash Malone took on the riders coming from the east while Fogarty's three mounted riders took on the others. It was heavy rifle fire from the freight wagon and the smaller buggy that turned the battle almost instantly.

Pasternak saw his mistake, wheeled his horse, and raced away from the bloody scene. "I see him," Calhoun yelled, spurring his horse into a fast gallop. "Come on, Squash." Malone saw and heard and spurred his horse into a frantic flight. Pasternak was headed for Gold Creek, probably hoping to get away through Dayton, several miles down the creek. Dayton was spread out along the Carson River.

Calhoun's arm and shoulder were hurting bad and he knew he wouldn't be able to keep up an all-out run for miles but wouldn't worry about it until he simply couldn't go any further. Squash Malone was alongside, and they were not gaining on the fugitive sheriff.

Bull Morrison got the wagons stopped and his force spread around him. "Check those bodies carefully, men. They may not be dead." He sent a couple of Monaghan's men and a couple of treasury agents to find the dead and wounded.

"Fogarty, Monaghan, join me, please." He stepped off his horse and walked to the small buggy. "Anyone hurt?" Sandy Ferris, Doc Watson, and Linda Bricky were okay, Morrison saw, but didn't see any movement from John Ivory or the wounded deputy. "Better check them, Doc. Don't look good from here."

Fogarty and Monaghan walked up. "Got a wounded man, Marshal," Mike Monaghan said. "Need some help getting him out of the wagon."

"Leave him right where he is," Doc Watson said. "I'll be right over."

Morrison squatted down on the side of the road and motioned for Monaghan and Fogarty to join him. "That was probably the last full attack we'll face, gentlemen. It doesn't mean we let down our guard. It'll be a long ride from Mound House to Carson City."

"I know how important it is to get these prisoners and all that gold safely back to Carson, Marshal, but I'm wondering if we might be better off staying at the switching yards for a day or two. Your two deputies are chasing the sheriff and their guns are important." Monaghan spoke the words that should have been coming from Fogarty.

"It's a toss-up, Mike," Bull Morrison said. "Those two guns are more than needed and getting all of this back in town is at the top of my list, but you do have a point. A good point. Fogarty's people are on left-over horses from the dead and wounded and aren't up to a hard chase across this great state of Nevada, and the wounded do need considerable attention."

Morrison stood up and paced about for a moment or two. "What's your thoughts, Agent Fogarty. Your people did right but I don't think you fired your weapon once. You've never been in a real fight, have you?"

Fogarty just looked at Bull Morrison, never saying a word. He certainly wasn't going to say anything about not firing his pistol or rifle, never going to tell this monster of a marshal just how terrified he was. Bull's glare scared him as much as the thought of being killed.

"Let's get moving to Mound House," Morrison howled. "After I talk with Doctor Watson and give all this some more thought, I'll make a decision. Let's move."

When the six men descended on the wagons, five were

knocked off their horses and one turned and ran. Of the five, four were dead and one seriously wounded. Of those riding with Morrison, only the one guard was wounded, and his wound wasn't that serious. Doctor Watson urged Morrison to hurry the caravan into the switching yards. "I've got help, there, Marshal. I'm afraid we'll lose at least two of these people."

Morrison agreed. "I've got to get wires off, too, Doc. Sure glad you were available. Is that Bricky woman giving you much trouble?"

"More than I want to remember. She's offered just about everything a woman has to let her get away. Good thing I'm not a young man," he laughed.

"HE KNOWS THIS COUNTRY, SLIM. We don't want to lose him." Squash Malone and Slim Calhoun were racing through heavy sage country toward the steep Gold Canyon with the creek in its bottom. "We gotta keep him in sight."

The Virginia Range flattened out at its southern terminus, and they were riding through rolling hillsides that ended at the Carson River to their south. The country hid deep ravines, rocky crags, up thrusts, and was pocked with ground squirrel burrows.

"He's got a good horse but he's not gaining on us." Calhoun almost chuckled thinking that just a moment or two before he lamented that they weren't gaining on Pasternak. "That's worked ground in front of us, Squash. Must be a ranch in the bottom of that creek draw."

Gold Creek Canyon hosted good bottom land for farming and ranching, and a roadway that led from Dayton to John Town. It rose along with the range up the mountain to Silver City. It was that creek that led the gold seekers to climb much higher and discover the Comstock Lode along the flanks of Mt. Davidson, often called Sun Mountain.

"If that's a ranch, then there are people about to face some serious trouble, Slim." Squash Malone urged his tired horse, stretched low on the horse's neck, and howled the cry of an Oglala warrior, while Slim Calhoun stayed as close to him as he could. They descended the side of the canyon onto the narrow valley floor and raced through good grass and sparse brush to a farmstead, less than a quarter mile in front of them.

Pasternak pulled his horse to a sliding stop in front of a large farmhouse, scattering a mixed flock of ducks, chickens, and geese, and bailed from the saddle. The commotion brought thirty-two-year-old Jeremy Wooster running from the barn, still holding the pitchfork he had been using. "Just what's all this about?" He shouted, running up to Pasternak.

"I'm Sheriff Pasternak. Two murderers are chasing me. I need help. Get a rifle or shotgun and help me." Pasternak was shouting at Wooster who saw two riders coming hard toward the ranch. "Hurry man, they've already killed my deputies."

Wooster was a law-abiding man from upper New York state. He brought his family west following too many horrible winters and lost crops. Gold Creek Canyon was developed over the years and the Wooster family thrived.

Jeremy dropped the pitchfork and ran for the barn, Pasternak right on his heels. Squash Malone didn't even attempt to slow his horse down but rode at a full gallop toward the running men, jumping from the saddle at the last instant, smashing into Pasternak at breakneck speed. The two rolled through the farmyard dirt and mud, crashing into the side of the barn.

Slim brought his horse to a sliding stop and found he was looking down the barrel of a shotgun held by Jeremy Wooster. "Far as you go," Wooster said. "Don't move."

"I'm Deputy U.S. Marshal Slim Calhoun. Easy with the shotgun. We're chasing Pasternak there for attempting to steal a gold shipment."

"He's the sheriff. Said you were killers. Got some kind of badge? Coz he does." Wooster had the barrel of the shotgun aimed at Calhoun's mid-section and Slim knew he could die at the slightest wrong move. Wooster's eyes and the way he held that scattergun told him all he needed to know. The man would pull the trigger. And worse, he believed what Pasternak told him.

"He is the sheriff but he's a crooked, outlaw sheriff. I'm going to slowly open my heavy coat and pull it aside. You'll be able to see my marshal's badge." He waited for Wooster to give him the nod.

"No, drop your gun belt first. Nice and slow. I don't want to shoot you, but I will."

Calhoun, with just the one good hand, pulled the belt free and let it drop to the ground. Two gunshots, almost fired together went off and Pasternak made a dash for his horse, jumping into the saddle and racing off down Gold Creek. "Damn," Calhoun shouted. He forgot about Wooster and the menacing shotgun and raced to where Squash Malone was staggering back to his feet.

"Here, Squash, lay back down. You're hurt bad." Calhoun eased the man down into the dirt, seeing blood flow from a wound high on the man's right side. "Probably missed your heart, but you're bleeding bad."

Wooster ran up with the shotgun in one hand and Calhoun's gun belt in the other. "Get me a pan of water and some clean rags, mister. Hurry." Calhoun had Malone's jacket and shirt ripped away and saw an ugly wound just below and to the side of the shoulder."

"You gotta get on the chase, Slim. Let this farmer take care of me. Get that bastard." Calhoun had Malone's shirt pressed hard against the wound, getting the flow of blood stopped as Wooster came back.

"Take care of him," Calhoun said, racing for his horse, strapping his gun on as he ran.

"My daughter will help you," Wooster said. "Let's get you in the house, get you cleaned up. You a marshal, too? Not a killer as the sheriff said?" He was looking into the face of an Oglala Sioux Indian who nodded that, yes, he was a U.S. Marshal. The long braided hair, dark complexion told Wooster one thing, but those burning blue eyes and a bright shiny badge told him something else.

Wooster had him on his feet and they stumbled their way across the farmyard and into a warm kitchen where Wooster's wife and teenage daughter were waiting. "Just sit in the chair and my wife and daughter will get you fixed right up. You don't look like a marshal."

Malone had to chuckle, thinking about that. "I guess I don't," he laughed. "I am Deputy U.S. Marshal Squash Malone and the other man is Deputy U.S. Marshal Slim Calhoun." The Wooster women were working on Malone all the time, and had the wound cleaned out but the bullet was still deep in the shoulder's flesh. Squash couldn't take his eyes off the young lady who was attempting to locate the bullet. "That does hurt a bit, ma'am," he said. She just smiled.

"The nearest doctor is down the canyon in Dayton," the other woman, Elsa Wooster said. "That bullet has to come out or you'll die of infection."

"Do you have a jug of whiskey?" Malone looked up at Wooster. The farmer nodded. "Get me loaded and pull the bullet."

"Oh, my," the young girl cried. "Oh, mother. No."

"It must be done," Wooster's wife said. "Get the bottle, Jeremy."

CHAPTER 22

FOLLOWING ON THE MAIN GOLD CREEK ROAD WAS EASY, EVEN AT A FULL gallop, but Calhoun knew that Pasternak had a long head start on this chase. He watched closely at the sides of the roadway just in case the outlaw sheriff pulled off. The roadway would dip into the long Dayton Valley, join with the main east-west immigrant road, and follow along the Carson River. His shoulder ached and he could feel the wound was open and bleeding again despite the good work by Doctor Watson. "Come on horse, we gotta catch that fool."

The canyon opened up into a broad plain, the creek flowing into the Carson River and the trail intersecting the main east-west immigrant road. Eastbound, the road followed the river to the little town of Dayton, which had hosted untold thousands of immigrants on the Carson Pass Road, searching for the illusive gold they'd heard so much about.

Calhoun saw the fresh tracks heading for the river, pulled his horse of up, and spotted the flash of a horse's flanks among cottonwood trees lining the river and jerked his horse in that direction. The horse and rider were moving quickly through the trees and brush, and Calhoun gave immediate chase.

"So, my fine outlaw sheriff, you're on the other side of the river, eh?" Making the ford was easy in the mid-winter. If it were spring, the river would be running hard. Calhoun picked up Pasternak's prints in the sandy soil and raced through the stand of cottonwood, willow, and sage, up a side hill and into rugged, rocky country. "There you are," he said, spotting the sheriff no more than half a mile in front.

Pasternak kept a close eye behind him, spotted Calhoun coming on fast, and spurred his big horse into a full gallop. Pasternak knew the narrow-gauge Carson and Colorado rails ran along the southern bank of the river, all the way to Fort Churchill, and hoped he could ride hard along the roadbed. Rolling hills spread out south of the river, and up the flanks of the Como Range.

If Pasternak could get high in the Comos, he would be safe. Rough, steep, rock filled country that climbed well over seven thousand feet would protect him.

The race was hard and fast, and Calhoun watched as Pasternak went flying over the head of his horse when one of the horse's front legs collapsed. Pasternak was on his feet, dazed, when Calhoun dove from his horse, driving the two of them into the rocks and dirt. Calhoun almost howled with pain when he tried to roll up on top of the thin sheriff, but Pasternak squirmed free, jumped to his feet and kicked Calhoun in the head, knocking him onto his back. The sheriff turned and ran toward Calhoun's horse but the deputy marshal was faster and tackled the man.

The pain from his wounded shoulder interfered with his fighting instincts and Calhoun, despite his overwhelming size, found himself almost outmatched. He head-butted, kicked, bit, and drove fists relentlessly as they tore up the sand and dirt. They rolled onto the rail bed, across the tracks, and Calhoun ended up on top of the man.

"You're mine, Pasternak. Give it up." Calhoun snarled. Pasternak answered by way of spitting at the marshal. "You lose," Calhoun said. He drove his fists, one, two, three times into the man's face, banging his head into the rail-bed each time, before Pasternak went limp.

Pasternak was finished and Calhoun got a set of hand cuffs on the man's wrists, Pasternak's hands behind his back. "On your feet, killer, move it now!" It was a long slow ride back to the ranch. Calhoun's horse was fine but the sheriff's horse had a distinct limp. "No broken bones, Sheriff. You're a mighty lucky man, gettin' caught by me. I know marshals who would have just as easily shot you, others would have made you walk alongside that injured horse. Not me, though. I'll get my pleasure a little later." They forded the river and were on the trail back to the Wooster ranch.

"I'm gonna enjoy watching you hang. Men who foul the honor of the badge die hard, Pasternak, and I'm gonna see to it that you do." Calhoun had to keep talking, first to ease the extreme pain from his now open wound, and two, to keep from passing out from a loss of blood.

Jeremy Wooster and his wife were on the front porch of their farmhouse watching the start of a winter sunset as Calhoun and Pasternak rode up. "How's that partner of mine doing? Can he ride?"

"You're bleeding, Marshal. Doubt that you can ride much further." Jeremy Wooster started to move toward him.

"No, stay back, please. This man is as dangerous as you've ever imagined. We have to get him back." He stepped down from his horse as Squash Malone and a lovely teen-age girl came out onto the porch. Calhoun wasn't aware just how badly injured he was. His knees were weak as he stood next to his horse, using it to keep up a front.

"Ah, Slim. Good work." Squash stopped suddenly as the full picture came into view. "You're bleeding bad, Slim." He turned to the girl. "Gladys, will you take care of my partner. I've got to take care of the prisoner. Mr. Wooster, can I beg you, sir, to take care of our horses. I'm afraid we'll be spending the night in your barn."

Gladys rushed down off the porch to Calhoun's side and took hold of an elbow to steady the man. Slim Calhoun wanted to argue but didn't have the strength. It was hard getting down from his horse, his knees were weak, and he saw blood dripping onto the ground from his wound. "Old Doc Watson ain't gonna like what I done to his handiwork." He could almost see the stitches ripped free and the blood pulsing through open flesh.

Gladys took him by the hand, and he found he didn't want to do anything but follow her, anyway. She had a quiet way of directing him up the stairs and into the house. "Let's get you in that chair and see if we can get your shirt off. My goodness what you marshals do to yourselves."

Squash ripped Pasternak out of the saddle, let him fall to the ground, and jerked him to his feet, slapping him hard with an open hand. "That's for shooting me, Pasternak. There'll be more coming." He pushed him hard toward the barn, appreciating how bloody and swollen the man's face was. You tenderized him up just fine, Slim. He won't be giving us any more problems.

Gladys Wooster had Slim's shirt off and was cleaning blood from the now open wound. "That's a gunshot, too," she whispered. "I fix papa's injuries all the time, but now I've fixed two gunshot wounds in the same day." She may have been only sixteen years old, but her eyes and smile were those of a woman. Her touch was velvet soft as she cleaned and dressed the wound. Calhoun's thoughts were far from reality as he enjoyed being tended to.

"You're pretty good at all this. Gonna make somebody a good wife." She just looked at him, smiled and kept right on trying to get him patched up. It amazed him that such a young girl knew how to sew up a man's wounds. He tried to smile through the pain, wanted to talk more with her, but kept losing track of where he was, what was going on. "You've lost a lot of blood, Marshal. Gonna need some good hot food in you to build it back up." She had him wrapped and tied and handed him his bloody shirt.

"Mama will have supper ready soon. You're not going to bring that other man into our home are you?"

"No," Slim said. "That outlaw won't be sullying your table or kitchen. We'll take our meal in the barn and be gone by first light. Thank you for this." He fought his way to his feet, had to hold on to the back of the chair, shook off Gladys's hand. "No balance," he muttered. He put his shirt on, slipped into his jacket and made his way to the porch. "My knees are still a bit weak, but I'm sure your mama's supper will fix that little problem."

"Horses are in stalls in the barn, Marshal," Jeremy Wooster said. "They're fed and wiped down. That one's got a nasty twist. Best to keep him quiet for several days. Marshal Malone lost a lot of blood and so did you. You're welcome to stay as long as you need. Sorry about the shotgun thing," he said. Wooster put his arm around his daughter and hugged her tight. "It would have been horrible if I'd shot you."

Calhoun laughed. "It goes with the job sometimes, Wooster. Your family has done good by us and we appreciate that. We'll be staying in the barn with our prisoner. Hope to be gone out at first light. We'll try to be quiet about it."

"No, you won't be eating cold biscuits out of your saddlebags, Marshal," Elsa Wooster said. "Gladys will bring you hot food just as soon as I get it all put together. And, I won't let you ride out without a hot meal in the morning, either. My goodness, with all your dangerous work, you must eat well," she said.

Calhoun was still smiling when he walked into the barn. Pasternak had his hands cuffed behind his back and wrapped around a barn post. He was sitting with his back to the post, a long rope wrapped tightly around him. "Well, now, outlaw sheriff, you look about as tied off as any calf I've run across. I guess it's time for introductions, eh?"

"I kinda went through that," Squash Malone said. "He doesn't like marshals."

"He say that?"

"Not using nice language, like we do," Squash said. "Got our bedrolls laid out over there. I have some elk jerky and hard biscuits, enough for the two of us. Hope you have coffee in your bags. Didn't look."

"Yeah, let's get some coffee going. Mrs. Wooster is bringing us hot supper, Squash. We'll leave the cold hard-tack for Pasternak." It took just minutes to get the fire built up in the barn forge and a pot of water boiling. "It's gonna be cold, Squash. We'll keep this fire going all night." Calhoun settled down on his bedroll, staring up at the barn's roof. "Gotta get this fool back to Mound House, Squash. Bull is gonna need our guns getting that gold and all his prisoners back to Carson City."

"With both of us shot up, we can't be kind to Pasternak. We get him on that crippled up horse of his, we gotta make sure he's tied down tight." Malone was pacing around the barn.

"You're worried about something, Squash. What is it?" Calhoun sat up straight and saw the big marshal rubbing his shoulder.

"They had a hard time getting the bullet out, Slim. I don't have a lot of feeling in my shoulder or arm. Can't move my arm much at all. Fingers don't want to work much, either. I'm not gonna be much help, is what I'm worried about."

"Well, when the time comes we'll get all upset about that, Squash. Some hot food, a good night's sleep, and you might wake up just fine. Here comes Gladys and her mother now."

"Prettiest girl I've seen in all my years," Malone said. Calhoun had to agree, but the way Malone said it caught his attention. Squash Malone had fallen for that girl, he thought. He watched as Squash's eyes were locked on the girl, and hers were locked on Squash.

The women had trays with three full meals and a large pot of coffee too. "Good hot food, boys. With all of you wounded and tired, you need a good meal. Lamb stew, fresh bread, and Gladys will bring some peach cobbler after. Oh, well, you've made coffee. Looks like this extra coffee will help." Elsa Wooster busied herself getting the food laid out and Gladys got a little close to Pasternak.

The sheriff reached out with his foot and tripped the girl such that she fell across him. Squash jumped up and pulled her off the man, reached down and smashed a fist into the prisoner's already bloody face. "Never walk up on a wounded prisoner, young lady. Never," he said. She jumped back from Squash like she'd been shot. He reached out and gently pulled her close, letting her cry.

"I'm sorry," she blubbered, and Elsa put her arms around her shoulders.

"You didn't have to yell at her," Elsa said. She was squeezing the girl's shoulders, rubbing gently.

"Ma'am, that's a killer there. I'm sorry if I frightened you, Gladys, but that's the most dangerous thing you could have done." She had her arms wrapped tightly around the big marshal, still crying. "He's all tied up and that's why you're safe. Please remember this for the rest of your life. It could save you big problems down the line." Squash gave the girl the best smile he could, hoping to ease her fright. Slim could see the fright slowly ebb, and she offered just a bare smile back.

He saw something else. Squash had feelings for this girl, and she was looking far deep into his flashing eyes. "I'm sorry, Squash. Thank you," she said. He took her dainty hand in his massive mass of muscle and bone, and they stood quiet for just a moment.

"Ain't no man or animal ever gonna hurt you if I'm close," he said. She stood as high on her toes as she could and gave Malone a gentle kiss on the cheek. "You'd best get back to the house, Gladys. Gettin' to be cold and dark."

The two women made a hasty retreat for the house and Slim Calhoun wondered just what they would be telling Wooster. "You scared her pretty good. Something going on there?"

"Yup." Squash walked over and slapped Pasternak again, just because he could. "It ain't gonna be the end of it, Slim. I don't think there'll be an end." Calhoun just looked at the man, not understanding at all.

"When this is all over, I'll tell you how it is, my friend."

DOCTOR WATSON HAD BEDS lined up along one wall of a long building he called his clinic. "You won't be hauling these people into Carson City for a day or two, Marshal. Serious bullet wounds, broken bones, burns that are already infected. It's only ten miles or so, I know, but you'll kill some of them."

Bull Morrison thought it would be best if many of them were dead, anyway, but his job came first. "I'm in a hell of a mess, Doc. My two deputies are chasing an outlaw sheriff somewhere east of here, I have wagons loaded with thousands of dollars of gold, eight or so wounded, and weaklings from the treasury department crying because they aren't being fed hot meals three times a day."

Watson was laughing hard by the time Morrison finished. "All the more reason to stay a day or two, Marshal. Why don't you send a wire to the sheriff in Virginia City? He could send deputies down to escort that gold into Carson City and you could stay and guard these wounded prisoners. By then, you might have word on your deputies."

"You make a strong case, Doc. You'd make a fine lawyer, you know. All right, then, we'll stay two days. I'll send a wire right away." He found Monaghan and had him round up Fogarty and the treasury people and slipped into the station house to send word to Virginia City that he needed help.

Fogarty, Monaghan, and the others were in the waiting room of the station when Bull Morrison came in. "The sheriff up in Virginia City will be here first thing in the morning with three deputies. He'll escort the gold wagons back to Carson City. Fogarty, you and your agents will ride shotgun." He glared at the agent, daring the man to say something. "Monaghan, you and your men will be in the wagons for protection.

"I doubt there'll be any problems, but it's best to have too many guns than not enough. Butch Endicott will stay here with me. Our prisoners are not in any condition to give us problems, but on the other hand they can't be moved just yet. Any questions?"

Fogarty started to say something, and Monaghan was louder. "I'll have the teams hitched and ready at first light, Marshal. There's a train work crew already on the scene at the wreck, and they said they will bring any gold or silver they find back here. I'm sure you'll see to it that it gets back to the mint."

"You bet I will," Morrison said. "You keep your men at the wagons overnight, Monaghan. You've done a fine job and I plan to see to it that Abe Curry knows that."

CHAPTER 23

"TIE HIS FEET UNDER THE SADDLE, SQUASH. I'LL LEAD HIS HORSE. The main road is just a short piece down the canyon here. I remember it but not a lot. We were riding hard and went the other way." Calhoun was chuckling as he struggled getting his horse saddled. "Hard work when you've only got one wing working. How's yours doing?"

"Better than yesterday. Got more feeling in my arm but no strength. Gladys did a fine job jerking the bullet out, but something got nicked during the surgery. I've never met anyone like her, Slim. She's as pretty as my mother and as strong as an ox," and he paused. "Well, enough of that. Has Pasternak said anything to you since you caught him or since he's been here? I ain't heard a peep out of him."

"Only a few words that I'd rather not repeat. He's a quiet one and those are the ones that spend a lot of time brewing up trouble."

"That's what's been going through my mind. You ride in front, leading Pasternak on the crippled horse, and I'll ride behind. If each of us has a rope around his neck, he shouldn't be any trouble." Squash Malone had his first fight of the day getting Pasternak in the saddle and his feet tied off under the horse. "You kick at me one more time and you're going

across the saddle for the whole damn trip back to Carson City."
Squash bashed the bruised and battered sheriff across the side
of the head and the outlaw sheriff quieted down.

"It's a short ride from Gold Creek to Mound House, Slim.
Sure didn't seem short when we were chasing this fool yesterday. I woulda swore we chased him for fifty miles or more."

Calhoun was laughing, remembering that mad dash across
the brush studded desert. He was also worried about getting
this prisoner back. "Neither one of us can use our rifles,
Squash. If we hit trouble, let's run as hard and fast as we can."

"Best plan I've heard," Malone laughed. "but it won't work.
That horse Pasternak's on couldn't run ten yards. No. If there's
trouble we'll just do what we always do. Win."

They walked their horses out of the barn, leading Pasternak on his. The Wooster family was on the porch, waiting for
them. "Morning, Mr. Wooster," Slim said. "Can't thank you
enough for taking care of us. Could have been so nasty. When
we get everything straightened out, you'll be receiving a letter
of thanks from the marshal service along with compensation
for your help."

"Oh, my," Jeremy Wooster said. "Didn't expect that. Es-
pecially since I almost shot you, Marshal. I can't really say
I'd like to do this again," he chuckled, "but if you're in this
neighborhood, you'll always be welcome."

"Your wife's a fine cook and your daughter's a fine doctor, Wooster. Take care of your family." Calhoun waved and
turned to lead off. Pasternak would be trailed, and Squash
Malone would follow behind.

Both of them gun-shot and a prisoner not hurt badly
enough. They could be in trouble. Don't think I'd make it as a
marshal. "I'm coming, Elsa," Wooster hollered after she called
out. "I can smell those sweet rolls clear out here."

Gladys stepped down from the porch and walked up to Malone's horse. "Will I ever see you again, Squash? I know we talked about it, but I don't like having to watch you ride off like this." Her big eyes were filled with love as she spoke. "I'm going to think good things about us every minute of every day."

"You'll see me again, Gladys. I promise you, I'll be back." He reached down and lifted her like a feather, kissed her gently, and set her back down. Old man Wooster missed it, so did Elsa, but not Calhoun. "Soon," Squash said. He kneed his horse and the three moved off.

"That was quite a goodbye, Marshal Malone."

"Weren't a goodbye at all, Marshal Calhoun. Just a 'see you later,' thing."

Calhoun had a questioning look on his face and Malone ignored him completely. "I'm not one to get in another man's business, Squash, but I have to know that your mind is on our current situation."

"It is, Slim. Our current situation is far more dangerous that what it is I would rather be thinking of, but I won't burden you with that. Everything will come to pass no matter how much time one puts into thinking about it. So, I won't think about it." Calhoun had to chuckle and put his mind to their current situation.

The Gold Creek trail intersected the main east-west immigrant road at the canyon's broad opening, and they turned west at the bottom of the hill. They rode up and over the top and could almost see the switching yards at Mound House when they topped out. "Seemed like we chased that fool for fifty miles yesterday, Slim." Malone was pointing at the smoke coming from a locomotive moving slowly up the tracks to where the wreck was. "Getting ready to clear the tracks already."

As they approached the main station, they saw Mike Monaghan getting his men situated in the freight wagons,

with Fogarty's men on horseback, and others, wearing badges, nearby. "Looks like they're gettin' ready to pull out, Slim.
Where's Bull?"

Two of the men wearing badges rode up fast. "Stop right
there," one said, leveling his shotgun at the three riders. "Don't
come another step."

Calhoun almost smiled. "This would make Bull Morrison
smile for a week," he murmured to Squash. "I'm Deputy U.S.
Marshal Slim Calhoun," he called out. "And this is Deputy
U.S. Marshal Squash Malone. This other critter is our prisoner, Sheriff Sam Pasternak. Before you shoot us, you better
let Marshal Bull Morrison know we're here."

"I was hoping it was you," one young deputy said. "Morrison said to keep an eye out for you. We're down from Virginia
City. Bull's in the train station and we're pulling out." The
deputy from the Comstock waved at Monaghan who got the
big freight wagons moving. "Glad you got that damn fool."

"HOPIN' I WOULDN'T HAVE TO SEND out a search party for you two."
Bull Morrison was having coffee with Station Master Small
and Doctor Watson. "Looks like you boys got into some rough
country." He took in all the bandages on his two deputies as he
paced around the three. "Good. The prisoner looks worse than
you. That's good, too. Gave you some trouble, eh?"

"He's quick to fight, quick to run, and quick to shoot, Bull,
but he gives up when it starts to hurt. I think we all need some
of your attention, Doc. The young lady at the ranch we stayed
at did a good job, but you better check us over some." Slim
Calhoun handed Pasternak over to Bull Morrison.

"He'll need some lookin' after as well."

They walked across the rail yards to where Doctor Watson

had a hospital set up. "Where do we stand, Bull? Looks like you got some help from Virginia City. Afraid Squash and I won't be a lot of help for a day or two."

"We ain't moving for a day or two," Morrison growled. He looked around and laughed, and started counting. "Lost count, but it seems that me and Endicott, oh, and you, too, Doc, are the only ones who aren't wounded or dying. God help us."

Morrison got Pasternak to a cot and started to take the cuffs off when he felt the man tense up. "You do what you're thinking. Go ahead. I haven't had any fun for two straight days now. Last real fun I had was whuppin' on old Buffalo Butch Endicott." He had a fist full of Pasternak's shirt with one hand and his other hand cocked back, ready to pulverize the outlaw sheriff's face.

"See those knuckles, Sheriff? You do what you're thinking, and I'll give you a personal introduction." Morrison felt the tightness go out of the man and laughed at him. "Tough guy, eh?"

Calhoun was laughing, walked up behind Pasternak and slowly took the cuff from one wrist. "On the bed," he said, pushing the man down. He whipped the man's arm up and latched the open cuff to the metal frame of the bed. He grabbed a set of cuffs from Bull and attached one end to a leg and other to the bed frame. "Don't anybody get close. He kicks, hits, and bites, just like the dog he is."

"I haven't seen that before, Slim." Squash Malone stood at the end of the bed. "His right wrist and left ankle. That boy's hog tied. Gotta remember that. I've always used one set of cuffs for each arm and each leg. You got him solid, and his working arm is the one bound down. Yes, sir, I'm gonna remember that."

"Let's talk plan, Slim. Doc can take care of you boys in a while." Morrison led them back into the station house. The wood stove was hot, and a fresh pot of coffee was boiling away. "We need a whole cavalry hospital unit to get these people back to Carson City. On top of that, the major wants a preliminary report pronto. We've been burning up the telegraph wires. Treasury people are yelling that we created the problem. I'm gonna shoot Fogarty when we get back."

"Got a list of wounded and injured? That's a starting point."

"Yeah. Ivory's all but dead but won't concede, and Bricky's just got that busted up leg. She was shot but it ain't no big deal. Pasternak and three of his deputies, along with Sandy Ferris, you, and Squash. Out of eleven, nine are wounded. Doctor Watson doesn't want Ivory and some of the others moved for at least another day."

"I see at least three wagons, then," Calhoun said. "We rest today and tomorrow, then pull out. Squash and I will be fine. Ferris can't ride but he can still shoot, and you and Endicott are fine. It'll be a slow ride back to town, but I don't see a problem."

"Yup, that's why you ride with me, Calhoun," Morrison said.

CHAPTER 24

"Got that face of yours banged up good. Who are you?" Linda Bricky was laid back on her cot, her broken leg in a cast and the wounds and burns well on their way to healing.

"Name's Sam Pasternak. You the woman tried to steal the gold? All you needed to do was put a hole in the tracks, not blow up the whole train."

"That was the plan. Partner got a little too much juice running through his system." She let out a slight and ironic chuckle. "That's his sad butt over there." She pointed to Ivory's bed across the room. "Why'd somebody pound on your face?"

Pasternak didn't like the question, didn't like the woman, even if she was good looking, and took a second to think about where he was and how to get away. Where would he go if he did get away? Some big city where he could disappear, change his name, and be safe. Chicago? St. Louis? San Francisco? Could she help? He sure as hell couldn't go back to Carson City.

"Those two marshals took a personal dislike to me." He offered just the slightest smile through fat and split lips, his black and blue eyes dull, unemotional. His mind was on two very important aspects of his future life. He had to disappear, that was a given, but in doing that he would be giving up the most lucrative life he had ever known. Warm Springs. There were three operating whore houses, two full gambling and dance halls, and the hot springs resort. And they were his.

Between those operations and the gang of thieves and murderers he ran from the resort's safety, Pasternak had more money that he had ever seen in his life. He would have to give that up. He had money and other valuable holdings tucked away that he would have to get his hands on, but first and foremost, he had to escape.

He's a cold one. Said Pasternak's his name. Is he the sheriff? Everyone said he was a bad man, but I wonder why he's here, chained to the bed? "Pasternak, eh? The Sheriff in Carson City is named Pasternak. Relative of yours?"

"That would be me," he said. "I need to get away from here and fast. I ain't going to jail. Ain't. Somebody help me, I could make it worth their while."

"Me too," she laughed. "I got to get out of here. They got us chained down tight, Sheriff. Got any ideas?" Linda Bricky had been trying to come up with a plan to get away ever since they chained her wrist to the bed. "I almost got my wrist free earlier, but that big bastard caught me. They call him Bull. I think he's sadistic, loves to hurt people." Bricky looked at the bruised and bleeding sheriff and almost laughed.

"If we did get away, that busted up face of yours would give you away no matter where we went. Me? I'm heading for San Francisco as soon as I'm a free bird. Big banks there, and if there's one thing I know, it's how to bust into big banks."

Pasternak wondered about that. She might know how to rob banks, sure doesn't know how to rob trains. San Francisco? My kind of city. Easy to get lost in a city like that. Have to come up with a name.

"That Marshal Morrison, Bull, is with the doctor when

he comes in to tend to us." Linda was talking to him and he better pay attention. "He has to unlock me so he can work on my wounds. Morrison never gets close enough for me to do anything. We need to get a key for these cuffs."

"Maybe you'll have to honey up to that ugly bastard."

She made as if throwing up but also wondered about that. That other marshal, the one with the longer hair wasn't bad looking at all. Doc had him patched up, too. "Not Morrison, but the one called Slim might end up in my sights," she chuckled.

SLIM, BUTCH ENDICOTT, Squash Malone, and Bull Morrison were sitting around a table in the station master's office, working on a plan to get everyone back to Carson City when Irene Thorndyke and Henry Honeycutt walked in.

"Must have been one hell of a wreck," Honeycutt said, shaking hands with Bull Morrison and getting a chair for Irene. "All anyone can talk about in Carson City. Glad you survived. Word is you have the sheriff in chains."

"Thanks, Henry, and yes we do. You out to view the remains? Many people out there searching for gold right now. Train people are chasing 'em off. No local law people out there, though. We killed or wounded all of them," he laughed.

Irene was looking at Slim's bandages. "Were you hurt bad, Slim?"

"Almost back to normal, Irene. What brings you out? Just looking?"

"No, we're here at Abe Curry's and the acting sheriff's request. The deputy, Tiny Beltram, has been named sheriff until an election can be held. He knew we were coming and asked us to bring him a report on Pasternak."

"Should have come himself," Morrison growled.

"Pasternak brought most of the sheriff's department with him. You have them in chains or underground, Marshal," Henry Honeycutt said. "Beltram only has two men left, one old man and a half-crippled jailer. Beltram's almost alone in the office."

"When are you planning on coming back, Slim?" Irene asked. "Curry wants to personally thank all of you for a fine job in getting the gold back to the mint. He says there's less than fifty dollars missing."

"One more day to get these wounds a little better healed, but we need to put together transportation. Everybody's busted up. The two who spend more time beating on each other than drinking beer are the only ones not wounded." He nodded at Bull and Endicott and got snarls from both of them. "We need a couple of fair-sized wagons to get everyone to town."

"I can handle that," Irene said. She walked out of the office and over to the station telegraph office and was back in minutes. "Wagons will be here first thing tomorrow morning, and Curry is sending Monaghan and one of his men as driver-guards."

"That's the kind of good news I like. Calls for a drink, I think." Morrison pulled a bottle from his large coat and took a drink, offering it around. "Good plan."

Slim Calhoun wrote a quick letter to Abe Curry, a report on the episode to that moment, and Irene and Henry were ready to head back to Carson City. "I think we might have a little party planning to do, Henry, for when these boys get back. Okay with you, Slim?" She kissed the big marshal and stepped onto her horse.

"Sounds like another fine plan. I like the way we party. Have a safe trip."

Back in the station house office, Bull was ready to plan out their trip back. "It's a short run, we'll have plenty of protection, and I'll be glad to be rid of these fine folks."

"Other than prisoners, we won't have anything of value with us, Bull. I don't think any of them are that valuable, that there would be an attempted attack on us." Neither Bull Morrison nor Slim Calhoun were aware of Sam Pasternak's Warm Springs holdings or the gang of outlaws he led. Their thinking on safe passage through the Carson River canyon would be different if they did.

SLIM WAS SITTING on a cot in Doc's clinic, letting Watson clean and re-bandage his wound. "Looks fine, Slim. No infection and it's healing good. No more wrestling matches until it's fully healed this time. You've ripped it open twice now. That's enough." Watson was smiling and giving the deputy just a little jibe or two.

'Ain't always my choice, Doc," Calhoun laughed. "Talk to that fool over there." He was pointing at Pasternak.

"He's not hurt that bad, Slim. Just multiple bruises and scrapes. No bullet or knife wounds. Be very careful around him. He's not hurt bad at all."

"He's that type. Feigning all kinds of hurt and jumping you when he gets the chance. Thanks for the warning. How about Linda Bricky? We might have to have them separated. She's a planner, and just as dangerous as he is."

"She was shot, and that wound is healing good. Her burns show some infection but will clear up overnight, and her leg is in a cast. She could walk on it if she was careful and could ride a horse."

"Need to keep close eye there," Slim said. "Maybe I'll have a little talk with her. How about Ivory?"

"He's hanging on. He lost a lot of blood, which is slowing the healing process. Yesterday I didn't give him much chance, but being inside, where it's warm, and with hot food, he's coming along. I don't think he's any kind of threat." Doctor Watson took a long breath and pointed at the two Carson City deputies.

"You got a threat there. Those two have scraped their wrists raw trying to get out of the manacles you've got them in. The one with the big bandage covering one eye spits when I'm even slightly close."

"Gonna be a mess getting these people back." Slim Calhoun motioned to Butch Endicott who was tending to Sandy Ferris. "How's he coming?"

"Gonna be limping some but he's gonna be fine. No bones broke, just his pride," he laughed.

"Tell me what you know about Tiny Beltram, Sandy. He's been appointed interim sheriff and only has two people working for him."

"Pasternak used to fire him every other week. Man's a good lawman. Glad to hear that. When Buffalo Butch gets through with me, I'm gonna try to walk. Gonna move everybody out soon?"

"Maybe," Slim said. He didn't want to give out a timetable in front of all the prisoners. Might give somebody some incentive. "Butch, help me move Bricky's cot. Gotta get her away from Pasternak. Don't want to put her near those deputies, either."

"Hang her from one of the cottonwoods out there," Endicott said. "More trouble than she's worth. That window over there don't sit square. Cold wind comes in. Put her under that window and maybe she'll catch pneumonia."

Ferris tried to stand up, used Endicott for a crutch and found he had no problem. "Let's put my cot over there where she is and move hers here. Don't think I can help, though." He took a couple of faltering steps and then a few more, having less trouble with each step. "I'll be fine."

Endicott jerked Sandy's cot away from the wall and walked

toward Linda Bricky. He grabbed the end of her cot and jerked it across the room, almost upsetting it once, and jammed it against the wall. She was howling as if in pain and Endicott ignored her for a moment or two then told her to shut up. "You don't know what hurt is, woman. Might be time to learn."

Calhoun moved Ferris's cot into place. "New cot mate, Pasternak. I think you know him. By the way, he's a badge carrying Deputy Marshal. He's authorized to shoot you on any perceived threat. Don't want to forget that."

Pasternak hadn't said three words to anyone but Linda Bricky since his capture and just glared, first at Calhoun, then at Sandy Ferris. "Glad to see you, Sheriff. Comfortable?" Ferris smiled and sat down on the edge of the cot. "Want to see my U.S. Marshal badge? Looking forward to slamming the cell door on you. They're gonna hang you, Pasternak, high in a tree."

Linda Bricky was trying to get straightened out in her cot and Calhoun pulled the blanket up for her. "I heard him say something about leaving out," she said. She was nodding toward Sandy Ferris. "Where?"

"Jail," Calhoun said. "Then court. Then the gallows. Lots of dead people out there, and you're responsible for all of them. Blowing up a train, killing the engineer, are the main charges, though. You and Ivory are sure to hang."

"I could make it worth your while if you'd let me slip away."

"No, I don't think so. You, my busted up little prisoner, ain't got nothing I want."

"Your loss," she said. She rolled over, cussing, facing the wall, and pulled the blanket up.

Calhoun had to laugh, gently, and walked back to where Ferris was sitting. "She's just as dangerous as this fool," he said, indicating Pasternak. "Spend some time walking around, Sandy. I'm sure we're gonna need you and your gun when we leave out. You'll have to be driving one of the wagons."

It was late night when Linda Bricky tried to get the attention of the two Carson City deputies. "Can you hear me?" She had to whisper it twice before one of the men responded.

"What do ya want?" It was the once called Masters. He had been hit in the side of the chest with a bullet and was bashed in the head with a rifle butt but wasn't feeling that bad. Masters was a heavy man and none of it was fat. He enjoyed showing off by lifting heavy barrels of beer and toting them around.

"Want to talk about trying to get out of this mess?" She asked. "I've got plans for some big banks in San Francisco and need a new partner. Got any ideas?"

"Yeah, I do. Kill 'em all," Masters laughed. "You're nuts, lady."

The other prisoner, the one with his head swathed in several cubic feet of bandage, moaned, and said he'd like to hear more. "Banks are where the money is, lady. Think you can get us out of this?"

"With a little help. I heard them talking and the three of us will be in one of the wagons with a driver and a guard. I heard them say we're leaving early in the morning. We'll talk more then."

Masters was also planning something, but he was a loner, didn't want anyone else involved, in particular a woman. He listened and knew that if they did start something it would be the right time for him to get away. I hope they come up with a splendid plan. One stop at Warm Springs to grab my poke and I'm out of this country. Maybe kill Kerrigan on the way. He should be helping us, and I know he's standing at the bar thinking it's all his now.

CHAPTER 25

BULL MORRISON HAD EVERYONE IN THE STATION HOUSE SEATED around a couple of tables pulled together. The big wood burning stove was lit and coffee was boiling. It was nearing zero outside and the wind was kicking up swirls of snow and ice. Endicott, Ferris, Squash, and Slim all had eyes on the marshal.

"This ain't gonna be a fun ride to town, boys. The outlaw sheriff, two of his deputies, Bricky, and Ivory, are all healed up enough to give us trouble. Bricky and Pasternak are the most likely to cause trouble, but those two deputies are big and mean."

"Irene is sending two wagons," Slim said. "How are you planning to separate the prisoners?"

"I was hoping you'd tell me," Bull laughed. "Can't have Pasternak with his deputies or with Bricky. On the other hand, I'd rather not have Bricky with the deputies."

Slim Calhoun looked around the room. "Pasternak and Ivory in one wagon with Bricky and the deputies in the other. That takes the sheriff out of play, but it sure does give Bricky a chance to start trouble."

"I can't think of any other way. We'll put her at the front of the wagon and the deputies at the back. Keep 'em separated."

"Remember what Doc Watson has been saying," Calhoun said. "Pasternak wants you to believe that he's hurt bad. He isn't. It's all surface stuff, bruises and scratches. He'll attack and we better be ready."

"I'm wondering about being attacked on the road." Sandy Ferris said. "Pasternak has a gang of thieves and killers at Warm Springs. We know the wagons hauling the gold back to Carson City weren't hit, but I sure wouldn't count them hitting us to free the sheriff."

"I've heard about this gang," Bull Morrison said. "Our best bet is to stay as sharp as possible, keep our prisoners locked tight and separated, and shoot first."

They decided that Calhoun's plan for the wagons was the best but when Mike Monaghan and a couple of the other teamsters arrived in the morning with the wagons the plan fell apart. The wagons were small buckboard type wagons. The people would be crowded in. Monaghan had the Virginia City deputies with him, but they said the sheriff wanted them back, pronto, and they had to get back up the hill.

"Well, then," Morrison growled. "We gotta make some changes. Wagon number one, with Bricky and the two deputies. Ferris, you ride on the seat with Monaghan. Slim, mounted, you ride on one side of the wagon and I'll ride on the other." Morrison laid out his plan. "Wagon two will have Pasternak and Ivory. Butch, you ride on the seat next to the driver and Squash, you ride your horse directly behind. Rifles, shotguns, and sidearms loaded and ready."

"We better not allow for much separation between the buggies, either." Slim Calhoun said. "I really hope we don't have any trouble on the road from Pasternak's people or any others, but we sure as all get out will have trouble from our prisoners."

"Let's get 'em out here and tied down tight." Bull Morrison

said. He walked over to the Virginia City deputies "Tell that sheriff of yours thank you. I'd love to have you ride back into town with us, but I know you can't."

"It's been interesting, Marshal," the lead deputy said. "Good to see Pasternak in irons."

BUTCH ENDICOTT AND BULL MORRISON were at what was wagon number two as Slim and Squash brought Pasternak out of the clinic. They hustled him into the wagon and Bull Morrison chained him to the seat. "That was almost too, easy, Slim." Morrison was ready for a fight and didn't like to be put off like this.

"Bring Ivory out and we'll lay him out across the back of the wagon."

Ivory was conscious but didn't have the strength to give any kind of fight and they carried him to the wagon, laid him out on a straw mattress, and Bull chained him down. "Now the fun begins, boys," Morrison said. "Sandy Ferris, you stand over there with your shotgun. Butch Endicott, over there with yours. You see anything gettin' started, end it." Both men nodded back.

"Okay, Slim, bring the two deputies out." One of them was still having trouble with his balance after getting hit a glancing blow to the head by a heavy lead bullet but seemed willing to fight at any moment. "Shoot 'em dead if they try anything."

"Intertwine their hands behind their backs, Squash." Slim was standing off to the side a pace or two, his forty-five cocked and ready as Squash Malone got the deputies on their feet. The one called Masters feigned a hurt leg but Malone got him standing anyway.

"Growl at me all you want, but you will be walking out there, or crawling on your belly like the filthy snake you are," Squash said. He jerked the man up right, prodding some where he knew there was a bruise or two. Masters wanted to fight back but the deputy he was chained with couldn't stand upright and Masters had to keep the two from falling.

Squash unlocked the handcuffs and put the man's hands behind his back to lock the cuffs back in place when the other man, the one with the gunshot to the head, kicked Malone in the back hard enough to drive him into the now un-cuffed prisoner. Calhoun stepped forward and drove the revolver into the man's head, knocking him out of the game.

Malone grabbed his prisoner and wrestled him onto the floor of the clinic but was driven off when the man whipped his arm around. The cuff was attached to his wrist and the other end clobbered Malone across his face, opening a gash and spewing blood on both of them. Malone drove his fists into the prisoner over and over until the man quit fighting.

Calhoun had his prisoner on his feet, hands cuffed behind his back while Malone tried to get Masters off the floor. He sat him on the edge of a cot and motioned for Calhoun to bring his man over. He shoved Masters' hands behind his back and before closing the cuff on the empty wrist, got it entwined in the other man's arm. "Wherever one goes, the other follows," Malone joked.

"I'll hustle these two out, Squash. Find Doc Watson and get that cut taken care of. It's a dandy."

"He wrecked my pretty face, did he? He'll pay for that."

The two prisoners had a hard time walking with their arms hooked together and behind their backs, and one already having balance problems. Calhoun pushed them out the door and they fought their way over to the wagon. "Gave you some trouble, did they?" Morrison chuckled. He handed the shotgun to Slim and manhandled the two prisoners into the wagon. "I'll get these two tied down. Where's Squash?"

"Got cut. Doc's fixing him up and then we'll bring Bricky out. This won't be the last from those two."

Calhoun walked back into the clinic, now almost empty. Linda Bricky smiled at Calhoun as he walked up to unlock her hands from the bed. "Last chance, big guy. I can sure make your life better."

Calhoun laughed and un-cuffed her leg. "Going to the hangman will make my life just fine, Linda. Up on your feet now and put your hands behind your back." He was amazed that she did as he asked, and he took her by the arm and led her out the door. "Last one, Bull. Squash will be along in a minute. In the wagon, Linda."

She started to climb in but the wrapping on her broken leg held her up. Morrison just grabbed her and threw her the rest of the way. "Give me your hands, woman," he snarled. "Gonna tie you tight."

"That hurts," she cried.

"Shoulda thought of that a long time ago, woman. Let's get this party underway. We got a long ten or more miles and it's gettin' late." One delay after another and Morrison was running out patience.

"Too bad for your hurt," he said again. "Sandy, climb up with Mike Monaghan and watch Pasternak. Butch, get in this wagon and keep that shotgun ready. As soon as Squash gets out here, we'll move out." He and Slim Calhoun walked to their horses.

"It'll be one of the deputies that will give us hell, Slim. I can feel it. I'll bet lots of money that I don't have that it will be the Bricky woman who starts it."

"I'm gonna go with Pasternak. He's a sneaky devil. Never talks but he sees everything, never takes his eyes off me when I'm nearby, and seems to be always listening."

"It's gonna be a long ten miles, Slim. Here comes Squash. Let's mount up and move 'em out."

As soon as the wagon started moving, Ben Pasternak began working to get his wrist out of the cuff. His left wrist had been injured in a fight a few years ago and was thinner than the right one, and he could feel just how loose the cuff was. With all the noise from steel wagon wheels rolling across a gravel bedded road, he didn't have to worry about being quiet. It would be his moving about that would give him away.

In the other wagon, Linda Bricky was doing the same thing, nodding from time to time to the one deputy who said he would help. That boy ain't gonna be no help at all. Head all bashed in, half unconscious, and probably just another stupid man. Her wrist hurt like hell, but she kept working the cuff loose and within fifteen minutes felt the metal fall away. She had to get her feet untied without anyone seeing her.

"I'm cold," she cried out. Butch Endicott turned in the buggy seat and looked down at her. There were blankets in the boot between his feet and the driver's, and he grabbed one, shook it open, and laid it across Bricky. "Thank you," she said. It was followed by a big smile as she pretended to snuggle into the blanket.

Endicott gave her a frown and turned back to the front. Linda Bricky immediately started work on the ropes holding her feet trying not to show any movement, but it was picked up by Deputy Masters and he edged a little closer to Bricky. He twisted around some, hoping to get his legs close to those hands of hers. "Can't get my hands free, though," he whispered.

"We need to be able to ride out hard with one of the marshals as a prisoner. They have the keys. My feet are free, let's start on yours," she said. The blanket was offering protection and she moved as slowly as possible, working the ropes loose.

PASTERNAK GOT HIS HAND out of the cuff and was quietly working to get the ropes loose. Everyone in the caravan seemed to be watching the road and those using it. The marshals made their way from the Mound House switching yard down to the Carson River. There was considerable traffic riding in their same direction, mostly from Virginia City to the mills along the river or to the state's capitol. No one was paying Pasternak any attention.

Despite all the eyes on the road, no one paid the least bit of attention to John Kerrigan, Pasternak's main man at the Warm Springs bordello/casino complex. Kerrigan had two men. Sydney Connor and Adolph Ciarra hidden with extra horses in the rocks near the Carson City entrance to the river canyon. He caught the deputy's eye as he rode by, gave just a hint of a nod, and kept going.

His head still hurt like crazy, but he had hope now, and rolled over, tried to get his partner's attention but the fool was too busy playing footsie with Linda Bricky to pay any attention. He was tied tight, woozy from his head wound, and decided to just wait for Kerrigan's attack. Maybe those two will be loose enough to help with the attack.

Pasternak was loose enough to make an attempt at escaping when Kerrigan rode by, seemingly ignoring everyone in the wagons. The outlaw sheriff saw the nod to where the deputies were tied up and simply laid back down to await the coming attack.

CHAPTER 26

SLIM CALHOUN RODE FORWARD ENOUGH TO TALK TO MIKE MONAGHAN driving the lead wagon. "Slow 'er down a bit, Mike. We need to keep bunched up tight." Monaghan nodded and slowed his horses down a little while Calhoun turned his horse and told the driver of the second carriage to keep up close to the lead wagon. He moved back alongside the lead wagon and just caught Pasternak moving a free hand under his blanket.

"Hold it up, Mike," he yelled out. He had his Colt out and cocked, aimed at the outlaw sheriff's head. "Ease that blanket back, Pasternak, as slow as cold molasses." Morrison saw the action, drew his weapon and fell back alongside the trailing wagon.

Bull Morrison motioned Squash Malone up alongside and told Bricky to pull the blanket aside. She refused and when Squash reached down to jerk it away, Deputy Masters jumped him, almost knocking the huge marshal from his horse. Malone pulled back on the reins with one hand and tried to fight off the prisoner with the other.

Morrison, calm as he could get, reached out with his revolver and knocked Bricky unconscious. He was on one side of a stopped wagon while Malone and Masters were fighting on the other side. He jumped from the saddle into the bed of the wagon, and then leaped the short distance onto the fight taking place on top of Squash Malone's horse.

The horse threw a fit, bucking hard, kicking, twisting, and finally trying to sun dance the three bodies who, were still fighting. Hooves slashed at other riders, smashed wood from wagons, and had traffic on the busy road at a standstill.

Three big men tumbled to the ground just as Calhoun grabbed the loose reins from the bucking horse. Masters couldn't run because of ropes tangled around his legs and Morrison pounded him in the head half a dozen times before he quit fighting back. Within seconds Morrison had Masters on his feet, picked the deputy up and flung him back in the wagon. "Put cuffs on one of his ankles and the other on the other deputy." Morrison had an arm around Masters' neck, choking the man. "I ain't lettin' go until you tell me he's secure." Masters was losing consciousness fast and Malone got him chained quickly.

"Let him go," Malone said. "He's nice and tight." Squash turned to Linda Bricky. "What are we gonna do with this one, Bull?" Bricky was about half conscious and trying to sit up, both hands free and the ropes around her ankles untied and hanging loose. She was trying to shake off the tremendous slam to her head from Morrison's rifle, and losing the battle.

"Escape artist, eh? Won't be again," he laughed. He wrapped a set of cuffs around the chains holding Masters to the other deputy, and attached them to Bricky's ankles.

"Gonna be a most uncomfortable ride back to town, woman." Instead of handcuffs, he tied her wrists together behind her back and then tied her to one of the seat brackets. "You ain't goin' nowhere, woman." He was chuckling to himself as he stepped back from the wagon.

"You're bleeding again, Squash," Morrison said. "We gotta get this circus to town. You're hurt bad, Calhoun's hurt bad, Ferris is hurt bad. Damn, but I'm gettin' riled." He looked at the pile of bodies all cuffed and chained together and had to laugh. "One more uprising from you idiots and I'm gonna shoot you one at a time with six bullets each."

The melee in the middle of a busy road caused a traffic backup that was starting to get loud. Teamsters hauling ore down from Virginia City had schedules to keep and a bunch of cowboys fighting in the middle of the road wasn't on their schedule. The horse throwing a fit didn't help things at all. Families moving from the east to California hadn't heard that kind of language or seen men fighting in public since leaving St. Louis.

Bull Morrison got back on his horse and let those around them know he was a marshal and had prisoners. They didn't care if he was president of Panama. "Get the hell out of the road," one teamster howled, cracking a bull whip over a team of oxen. Pasternak took that opportunity to attack Slim Calhoun. His hands were free but with handcuffs dangling from one wrist, and his feet were too.

He leaped at Calhoun, hoping to knock him from his horse, but Calhoun saw it coming and drove his revolver down on the man's bruised and still sore head. Pasternak fell to the ground but was fighting to get to his feet. Calhoun leaped on him immediately. Using both a fist and the Colt, the deputy marshal whipped Pasternak unconscious and bleeding.

Ferris climbed down from the wagon seat and helped Calhoun throw the sheriff's unconscious body back in the wagon. "Ripped your shoulder open, Slim. They ain't gonna be nothing left to sew up if you keep rippin' it open."

"Bastard," Slim Calhoun said. He was helping Sandy Ferris get Pasternak tied off since he could slip out of handcuffs.

"Need five more people," Slim muttered. He eased his wounded arm inside his coat, taking pressure off the wound.

Morrison growled, "Let's get moving. Keep it tight and shoot the first bastard to start trouble. Let's step out lively, now. We've given these people a fine show." Teamsters were howling, yelling serious threats as they drove their teams past them, and children were horror stricken with the bloody faces of the prisoners staring back at them.

Squash got his horse back under control after its performance and rode around the wagons to make sure everything was still connected. "Lead off Sandy before some of us bleed to death."

"Just one hell of a show," Calhoun chuckled. "What the hell else could go wrong after all this?"

CHAPTER 27

"THEY'RE ABOUT A MILE BACK IN THE NARROWS," JAKE KERRIGAN SAID. He was up in the rocks with Connor and Ciarra. "Lots of guns, but our little surprise should take out most of them. Shoot the men on horseback first, then the wagon drivers. The sheriff's in the first wagon, Masters and Johnson in the second."

"Sheriff busted up bad?" Sydney Connors had gotten the word from a visitor to the hot springs that the sheriff was in custody.

"Looked like the marshals we heard about worked him over pretty good. They should be coming around that bend shortly. I saw Masters. Don't know who else might be in those wagons. It's important that we not leave any witnesses, boys. We gotta protect Pasternak."

The three gunmen rode down out of the rocks and hid behind an outcrop just off the main roadway. Kerrigan looked downriver and spotted the wagons coming on slow less than a hundred yards away. "Let's ride," he howled out, racing onto the roadway, Connor and Ciarra right behind.

Calhoun spotted the charge first, knew instantly what it was, and started firing before anyone else even knew there was a threat. Sandy Ferris raised his rifle and killed Kerrigan's horse, throwing Kerrigan face first in the rocks. Connor saw

Morrison coming at him fast, that double barreled scatter gun about to come in to play, turned his horse and ran, Ciarra right behind him.

Morrison rode hard but Connor's horse was much faster as it wove through traffic on the main highway. Morrison couldn't shoot while racing for fear of killing or wounding innocent people on the road. He pulled up and rode back to the wagons.

Kerrigan got to his feet as Ciarra rode up and with help jumped up behind the outlaw. "Ride hard, Ciarra," He yelled. Ciarra had his horse at a full gallop, going the other way, weaving in and around traffic, moving quickly down the river canyon. "Make for the hot springs," Kerrigan yelled.

Calhoun started to give chase but thought better because of the amount of traffic. Sure as hell someone would get hurt he thought.

"ANYBODY HURT?" Slim Calhoun reined up, looking back at Morrison and the wagons. He wanted to follow the outlaws, run 'em down, shoot 'em dead, but also knew there might be more of them, and stayed to protect his prisoners. "You and your big mouth, Bull," he shouted.

"What are you talking about?" Morrison rode up next to his deputy. "What big mouth?"

"I distinctly heard you say, 'what else can happen?' Didn't you? You know you did."

"It was you that said that," Morrison snarled.

Both men had to laugh as they rode back to the wagons. "Recognize anyone one, Sandy?" Morrison asked.

"Those were Pasternak's gang from the hot springs. Kerrigan is the one that splashed on the road, the others were Sydney Connor and Adolph Ciarra. They never got a shot off, Marshal."

"Yeah, you won that round, Sandy. Squash, help me move this dead horse off to the side and then let's get this show on the road."

They stayed bunched up tight as they made their way out of the canyon and onto the almost flat Eagle Valley. They still had about five miles to go before reaching the relative safety of Carson City.

It was Masters who saw the irony as the scene unfolded. "All we had to do was wait," he murmured. "We would be free right now if we had just waited." Masters didn't realize that Pasternak didn't initiate the attempted escape. Pasternak simply gave away the attempt and if he hadn't got caught, the escape surely would have played out differently.

"That won't be the last attempt, Slim." Bull Morrison rode up alongside his deputy. "After we get these yahoos in cells, we're gonna have to have it out with Fogarty and find out what we can about this Warm Springs complex. Sounds to me like the sheriff ran a gang of thieves from out there."

"I'm sure Irene or Henry Honeycutt can tell us all about it. We need to get some of these people to a hospital."

"To hell with that," Morrison said. "A doctor can come to them. They all need to be behind solid steel bars. I need a drink and a good fight with somebody. Maybe even a bowl of chili."

Calhoun was laughing hard when Squash rode up. "Bricky's bleeding hard, Bull. Maybe have to stop for a minute, get her bandaged."

"I'd rather just let her bleed to death," Morrison said. "Okay, let's find someplace where we can at least get out of the traffic lanes. We've caused enough problems for these other people."

Calhoun led Mike Monaghan off the road and into rolling hill and open country. "Gotta mend one of 'em," he shouted. "Keep a close eye on that outlaw sheriff while we work on Bricky. Any movement at all from John Ivory?"

"I'll check on him, Slim," Sandy Ferris said. He jumped down from the wagon and held his rifle at the ready, expecting anything to happen. Calhoun noticed a serious limp as Sandy Ferris made his way to the back of the wagon.

"Better see a doc when we get to town. Your hip giving you hell?"

"I'da been better off in a saddle than that hard seat up there," Ferris laughed. "I'll be okay. Just stiff." He shook Ivory and got a response from the man. "He's still alive, Slim. Only one who hasn't given us any trouble."

"Yet," Calhoun snickered. He rode to the second wagon and stepped down from the saddle. "So, Bricky, what's your problem now."

"She tore her wrist open on the ropes, Slim. Bleeding hard." Squash Malone had her arm free and was holding a bloody rag tight to her wrist. She appeared about half conscious.

"She playing sick on you, Malone?"

"Not this time. She's almost bled out."

"Okay," Calhoun said. He looked up at Morrison who just shook his head in disgust. "Tie that bandage tight and move her to the front of the wagon and chain her feet to the wagon. Let's get into town as quick as we can. What a damn mess."

CHAPTER 28

IT WAS A DEBATE AS THEY MOVED SLOWLY THROUGH THE OUTSKIRTS OF Carson City on whether to take the prisoners to the hospital or to the jail. "They need to be locked up tight. We can call a doctor to come to the jail." Bull Morrison was adamant, Slim Calhoun was on his side, and it was Butch Endicott who wanted the prisoners at the hospital.

"We know how well you've treated our injured and wounded, Butch, but it's just too dangerous to not have them behind steel bars. They've already tried twice today to escape, to hurt people. They need to be locked up and that's where they're going." Morrison rarely had to be the boss of an operation, but this time he had to.

It was quite a procession that arrived at the Ormsby County Jail. All of the prisoners had some sort of injury or wound, and half of Morrison's squad were wounded or injured. Tiny Beltram walked out to welcome them. "Sure wish I could have given you some help, Marshal. Right now, it's just me and old Spike, my jailer, keeping order in this city." He looked in the wagons and just shook his head.

"The sheriff and two deputies tied up like hogs at slaughter. Where are the others, Marshal?"

"Six feet under, Sheriff. He had five deputies with him and now you have two of them. There's also a dead railroad engineer, and some seriously wounded lawmen. These are my prisoners, Sheriff, and I'm turning them over to you and asking for good care until we can get court processing underway."

"You've got it Marshal." Tiny Beltram wasn't tiny. He stood well over six feet and weighed somewhere close to three hundred pounds. Rumor was he could eat four pork chops with mashed potatoes and gravy for each meal daily and still be hungry at bedtime. He reached in the lead wagon and grabbed Pasternak by his coat collar and jerked him out of the wagon. Beltram held him up high, the former sheriff's feet off the ground, as if to be inspected before an opening bid.

"Spike." Beltram howled, and a spindly old man hobbled out from the jail. "Let's get this fool locked up in cell number three."

Morrison was about to say something about turning over the dangerous Pasternak to a crippled old man who couldn't possibly fight back when Spike slipped a wire noose around Pasternak's neck and pulled it tight. "Let's go, Sheriff," he said, nudging the still bloody man into the jail.

"There's something you don't see every day." Morrison was laughing right out at the scene, and pointed at Masters, in the second wagon. "You're next, tough guy." Calhoun prodded the two deputies and Linda Bricky from the wagon, their feet entangled in sets of leg cuffs, ropes, and hand cuffs.

Bricky was too weak to stand up and Squash got her loose from the rest. "Along with the others, she's gonna need a doc right away, Sheriff." Beltram nodded and watched Malone carry the woman into the jail.

Sandy Ferris crawled down from his wagon seat to help. "You don't look so good, Sandy, Beltram said. "Ain't never seen you limp like that."

"Ain't never been shot in the hip, Tiny. Keep that in mind. It ain't a good place to be shot."

"Don't know how you got messed up in all this, but I just happen to have a job opening right now." The sheriff laughed, looking around at the mess of wounded prisoners. "I need three or four more deputies, as a matter of fact."

"I would love to have my old job back, Tiny, but how long are you gonna be sheriff?"

"Depends on whether you help me get elected in the special election next month." Tiny Beltram was laughing, shoving a mixed line of prisoners toward the jail.

"I'll run your damn campaign," Ferris laughed. "Watch out for that Bricky woman and for Masters. They've caused a lot of trouble getting back here today. Will those goons Pasternak calls security at the whore house cause trouble?"

"I've been expecting it ever since we got word of the train wreck. The sheriff and his men rode out mighty fast. Don't know if they swung by Warm Springs. Might want to tell that marshal about them."

"We already met them," Ferris said. He told Beltram about the attack and escape by Kerrigan and his henchmen. "Kerrigan got his horse shot out from under him, but nobody else got hurt."

"It will be my pleasure to shut that place down," Beltram said. "Might be my first official piece of business. Might also get me elected sheriff." He moved his bunch of prisoners into the jail building, prodding them, pushing hard at every chance.

Ferris helped Butch Endicott ease John Ivory from the wagon as Morrison walked up. "As soon as these yahoos are safely locked up, I have business with a certain representative of the treasury department, but I want Slim and Squash to ride out to Warm Springs and close it down. You said those men were Pasternak's gang? Want to ride out with Slim and

Malone?" Morrison was smiling as he asked.

"Beltram asked me to take my badge back, Marshal. I would love to represent the county on that ride. Pasternak has created enough problems for Ormsby County and Carson City. I'll let Tiny know. He's a good man, Marshal. Make a fine sheriff."

"I'm glad to have had you on our team, Sandy. You'll do fine with Beltram." Morrison headed for the mint building and a meeting with Abe Curry and one Treasury Agent Fogarty. One could almost see the steam rising from the marshal's bulk as stormed across Carson Street.

"He'll want to have a good tussle when he gets back," Butch Endicott said. "Think I'll wait for him at the Palace Club."

CHAPTER 29

"I HAVEN'T HAD A BEER TASTE THIS GOOD SINCE WE RODE OUT OF TOWN several days ago," Slim Calhoun said. He was sitting at the end of the bar at the Palace Club, Henry Honeycutt on one side and Butch Endicott on the other. Irene Thorndyke served the beer. "Gold is safe, bad guys and girls are locked up, and the only point remaining is whether or not I'll have to arrest Bull Morrison."

"Why would you do that?" Irene was startled by the comment, stepped back quickly from the bar, almost glaring at Calhoun. "That would be terrible."

"What would be terrible, dear lady, is if Bull gets excited and shoots Fogarty twelve or thirteen times. He was in a rage the last time I saw him. In case you didn't notice, I've got his gun belt looped around my shoulder. He was afraid to wear it for his meeting with the agent."

"Morrison said something about Fogarty filing a complaint against him." Butch Endicott looked bewildered, saying that. "I don't understand at all."

"It's all politics at its finest, Butch. One government agency at odds with another, neither willing to give half an inch. Bull Morrison is a lawman in the marshal service. Fogarty is a bureaucrat in the treasury department. Water and oil, Butch.

They don't need stirring."

Sandy Ferris walked in and ordered a beer. "Beltram gave me the okay, Slim. We can ride out to Warm Springs anytime. I have warrants, if we need them." He was wearing an Ormsby County Deputy Sheriff badge. "Didn't take that judge half a minute to issue the warrants."

"Good. We'll use them. What are we looking at out there? Sounds ugly." Calhoun remembered Irene talking about the thugs on Pasternak's payroll and how they took pleasure in intimidating the weak. "This so-called Warm Springs gang of Pasternak's are the same men who tried to attack us on the road in? They turned tail and ran. Don't sound like no fierce gang to me."

"They won't run out there. There are four men who swagger about, threatening anyone and everyone, whupping on the women who work there, and taking most of what they make. They are always together. That's their power, just brute force." Ferris wanted to forget the first time he fell under their form of force. Ax handles and boots changed his mind about arresting one of them for assault. "They take great pleasure in hurting people."

"Sounds like a bunch of bullies, Sandy. Usually a gang of bullies will have a leader. Who do we go after first?" Calhoun asked.

"The one to watch out for," Irene said, "is called Jake Kerrigan. He's a big man and you're right, he is a bully. The others do what he tells them to do." She wrote down the names, leading off with Kerrigan's and handed it to Slim. "Sam Peters is a skinny little brute, but the one who might give you the most trouble is Adolph Ciarra. He's a knife man, sneaky bastard, who'll put a dagger in your back in an instant."

"Drink 'em down, boys. Let's take a little ride," Calhoun said. Endicott, Ferris, Squash, and Calhoun trooped out to their horses, leaving Irene and Honeycutt in the warmth of the saloon. "Wind's cold, and it's gonna be mighty late in the day when we get there, boys. They might have darkness on their side."

"Are we looking to make arrests, Slim? I heard you say something about closing the complex down." Squash Malone was riding alongside Calhoun.

"Our main purpose," he said this with a sly grin, "is to close Warm Springs, which I hope will get these noble outlaws all riled up and we'll be forced to arrest them. On the other hand, if I recognize some of the men who attacked us, and I know what two of 'em look like, we will arrest them no matter what."

"Yeah, I got a good look at one of them," Malone said. "Shame there were so many people around. Didn't dare take a shot at any of them."

"MR. CURRY, we've filled the jail and you have your gold and silver safe," Bull Morrison said. He was ushered quickly into the grand office. "I need to find that fool Fogarty and get some things straightened out."

"Read this before you confront the man, Marshal. I also want to take this opportunity to thank you for your fine work. I've sent letters to the marshal service and to the treasury department telling them what a fine job you and your deputies did." Curry handed a letter that he received from treasury agents in San Francisco. "You won't like this."

Morrison scanned the piece and handed it back. "I got word of this from our San Francisco office when I got back to town. Small minds, Mr. Curry, create the most trouble. I'll let those who run the marshal service deal with those who run the treasury department. No, sir, I'm not here to get involved in petty bureaucratic shenanigans, I'm here to educate."

Curry had heard all the talk about Bull Morrison living for the next fight and he finds a philosopher standing in front of his imposing desk. Bull gave the best impression yet of a real smile, turned, and walked out of the office. "It's been a pleasure working with you, Curry."

He found Fogarty and two of his agents in their little office near the vaults. "Have that gold nice and safe, do you? Well, I'm pleased. I'm a fair and decent man, Agent Fogarty, one who took my oath of office with a feeling of warmth and pride. I want you to be aware that you put yourself in a most dangerous situation for no reason other than pride. You also interfered with an investigation being conducted by the U.S. Marshal Service. That, sir, is a high crime punishable by many years in federal lock-up."

"I'll leave that to others, Fogarty. Your best bet is to be on the next train east and hope your fellow bureaucrats will protect you when you get there. My charges have been filed. Have a most unpleasant journey, sir."

Bull Morrison strode from the mint building with just one thought in his mind. I really wanted to shoot that bastard. Calhoun will never believe how I acted, and I'll never tell him. There was a soft chuckle to his voice as he asked Irene for a cold beer. I'm not the man you thought I'd be, Slim Calhoun.

JUST AS CALHOUN SAID, it was getting late in the day, the wind was coming straight out of the north and carried bitter cold deep into Calhoun's posse as they rode the short distance from the heart of Carson City to Warm Springs. The Sheriff's resort of houses of ill repute, hot mineral baths, and gambling halls, was already lit as they rode in. Slim led Squash Malone, Sandy Ferris, and Butch Endicott to what was apparently the head building of the small resort.

"Butch, keep a close eye on the horses and our backs. If we get company coming from behind us, you give a loud yelp and be prepared for war. These guys are dangerous. Squash, kind of hold back as Sandy and I introduce ourselves."

Of the four big men about to challenge the Warm Springs gang, only Butch Endicott was not suffering gunshot wounds, ripped stitches, and busted up hips. Sandy Ferris had a distinct limp climbing the stairs to the elevated porch, Squash and Slim both nursed painful gunshot wounds, and all four were looking forward to a good fight.

The enclave was laid out in a semi-circle, with the main brothel and gambling hall in the center. On the left flank were the hot mineral baths, and on the right were smaller, more informal saloons and gaming palaces, offering all the pleasures of the flesh. Slim and Sandy walked up the short stairway and through bat-wing doors into the main casino.

Music and loud voices permeated the air, along with a heavy cloud of cigar smoke. Red was the dominant color, in lamp shades, in velvet curtains, in table linen, and in the aprons the barmen wore. "Gaudy," Slim whispered. He walked up to the bar and asked the barman where he could find Jake Kerrigan or Sam Peters.

"Table in the back," the man grumbled, nodding toward a line of gambling tables that were set against the south wall of the building. There were five tables lined up, some for poker and faro, some for other games. Kerrigan was dealing five-card to a full table.

"I see him," Sandy said. "He's the one with the black hat, white shirt and red vest. Must be dealing tonight. That's Sam Peters sitting across from him. Sydney Connor is standing with his back to the wall in the black shirt and black vest. I don't see Ciarra."

"The man dealing is the one who started the charge and turned tail when I made my attack. Kerrigan, eh? He's mine, Sandy."

As Slim started back toward the table he saw Squash Malone come in and ease his way to the bar. "Keep several feet from me, Sandy, and watch Connor." Sandy Ferris eased back and edged closer to Connor as Calhoun walked up to the gaming table. There were four players including Peters.

"Are you Jake Kerrigan?" He asked.

"Who wants to know?" The dealer growled. He let his hand slip off the table and rest near his weapon. His eyes were pinpoints, shrouded by heavy lids and he had an ugly smile as he surveyed Calhoun. The word malevolent passed through Slim's mind along with coward, remembering how the man had turned and run off.

"I'm Deputy U.S. Marshal Slim Calhoun. You're under arrest. Stand up nice and slow and lay your weapon carefully on the table. Sam Peters, you do the same thing. You others at the table, vanish while you can." The three players moved quickly back from the table and Sandy motioned for them to move toward the bar.

Slim Calhoun was sure that Kerrigan would go for his gun and was surprised when it was Sam Peters who jumped to his feet pulling his Colt. Calhoun's lone shot exploded the man's heart, and Kerrigan found himself looking down the smoking barrel of a hot Colt. "Easy now, Kerrigan. There's no reason to die. How's your face feeling? That was a nice face-plant you made on the highway earlier today." Slow recognition crossed Kerrigan's face and he wanted to grab that revolver and found he couldn't. Fear is a strong visitor.

Sydney Connor spotted Sandy Ferris as soon as he and Calhoun walked in and wasn't surprised that Ferris made his way toward him. As Calhoun killed Peters, Connor went for his gun and fired one shot at Sandy, hitting him in the left hand, knocking him off his own shot. Connor raced for the front doors, firing behind him wildly.

There was instant chaos in the saloon as men either ran for the door or tried to hide behind anything that didn't move. Tables were turned over with men behind them, barmen found men trying to hide behind the heavy bar. The doorway was clogged, bullets were flying, and fragile oil lamps were exploding.

Ferris's hand hurt like hell, but he brought his weapon up and fired two quick shots at the fleeing Connor, missing both shots. Malone stepped from the bar, his Colt in one hand and a big Bowie knife in the other. As Connor raced for the doors, Malone slammed his revolver across the man's head, driving him face first into the filthy saloon floor.

Connor was strong and rolled when he hit the floor, right through the bat-wing doors and down the stairs into the mud of the open street. Malone was right behind him and dove into the mud, on top of the outlaw. Connor fought hard but Malone was able to get him rolled onto his stomach and pressed Connor's face into the filth.

Malone was heavy and held the thrashing Connor's face in the mud until there was no movement. As he slowly got to his feet, he felt a bullet slam into his leg, knocking him back down. Two more shots rang out, one aimed at Malone but missing. The second shot came from Butch Endicott and was aimed at Adolph Ciarra, hiding behind a water trough.

"He's behind the trough over there," Endicott yelled, firing again. Malone, despite his leg wound, crawled behind the porch stairs. There were tethered horses between where he was and Ciarra and Malone used them to crawl further down the line. Endicott watched him, understood what he was doing, and put another couple of shots toward the water trough.

"I'm gettin' damn tired of being a target," Squash Malone snarled, tying off a bandanna around his bleeding leg. "Gonna kill me an outlaw real soon."

In the meantime, Sandy Ferris, bleeding heavy from his hand wound, was helping Slim Calhoun get Kerrigan in irons and toward the front doors. Several patrons were starting to get involved when Calhoun fired his weapon straight up. "I'm a federal marshal. You want to get involved? You'll hang right alongside him. Now, back off or die." He yelled it out, brandishing his weapon, nodding to Ferris, who also had his gun out and cocked. They moved cautiously toward the big doorway but didn't go through.

The gunfire outside was constant and Calhoun forced Kerrigan to his knees and knelt down alongside the outlaw. He watched as Malone moved through the shadows toward the water trough where Ciarra was hiding. Endicott kept up a steady barrage, keeping Ciarra down in the mud. Malone had a good shot from off to the side and took it, knocking Ciarra flat. The bullet entered the man's side, piercing his lungs and heart.

Ciarra thrashed for just moments before giving it up and Malone hollered it was all clear. He dragged Ciarra's body and laid it out next to Connor's. "Take this man out," Calhoun told Ferris, and he walked back to drag Peters' body out with the rest. A group had formed on the porch surrounding the front of the saloon and Calhoun spoke to them.

"When Pasternak or Kerrigan isn't here, who's in charge?"

One of the barmen piped up that it would probably be him. "I'm Johnny One-Shot, Marshal. I guess that would be me."

"Well, Johnny One-Shot, you've got your work cut out, now. Pasternak is in jail and will soon hang, and as you can see, Kerrigan is in irons. By mutual order of Ormsby County Acting Sheriff Tiny Beltram and the U.S. Marshal Service,

Warm Springs is officially closed. You've got twenty-four hours to close 'er down, Johnny. Where'd you pick up that name?"

"People get out of line, that's all they get. One shot," he laughed. "What do we do about gettin' paid? Girls aren't gonna like not gettin' their share."

"Divvy up what's available and lock the doors, Johnny. Get us a wagon and team to get these bodies back to town. You men who don't work here, go home. This place is closed."

There was a lot of grumbling, but seeing dead and wounded scattered about, nobody was willing to make trouble. One of the barmen came racing out on the porch. "Fire," he howled. "Lamps got shot up and the place is going up."

"There's a wagon and horses behind the hot springs, Marshal. I'll have someone get 'em put together for you." Johnny One-Shot turned and started organizing a bucket brigade, called for everyone to pitch in.

"Ain't gonna save that old wooden building," Slim said. "Best try to get what you can out of there."

"All that money behind the bar," Johnny cried, running for the doorway. "Ain't nobody taken it to Pasternak for two days." He got almost as far as the batwings when little explosions could be heard inside.

"Bad whiskey adding to the problem, Johnny. Might as well say goodbye to the money and the building." Calhoun could hear bottles popping, barrels breaking open, and timbers creaking along with the roar of a major conflagration. "Goodbye Warm Springs."

"Gotta get the girls out," Johnny said, racing to the other buildings, screaming "Fire," as he went. Calhoun just shook his head, moving the posse and dead bodies back away from the fire.

Endicott was working on the wounded, stemming the blood from Ferris's hand wound, and getting a bandage tied onto Malone's leg. "I've been more of a nurse than a stone mason for days now," he said, making Malone gasp as he poured whiskey on the open wound. "You boys'll be fine as soon as we get back to town. Have to get that bullet out of there, Squash."

Johnny One-Shot had two men harness a team and get it hooked to a wagon, then helped Calhoun get the bodies in the wagon. Kerrigan was chained to a seat bracket and Squash Malone drove the wagon with his horse tied behind. Ferris was able to ride. What was left of the Warm Springs complex was still raging and a few men were working to salvage what they could.

"I don't anticipate any trouble getting back to town, but just the same, I'll lead and Sandy, you and Endicott bring up the rear. Everybody, keep your eyes and ears open." A few of the customers of Warm Springs were still grumbling, but with three dead men as proof of the abilities of the posse, there was no ruckus. They dispersed for their homes or saloons in town while Johnny One-Shot continued trying to save what he could.

It was the working girls doing most of the grumbling. They were out of a job, weren't sure they would be paid for what they had already done, and probably had no open options. "Hate to see things like this," Squash Malone said. "A lot of people out in the cold tonight because of that fool sheriff. I've been shot twice because of him, Slim. I'm starting to feel like Bull Morrison. I feel like riding back to town, walk in that jail, and shoot Pasternak twelve times."

CHAPTER 30

THE COLD WIND WAS HOST TO HEAVY SNOW BY THE TIME CALHOUN LED his posse back into town. He rode straight to the jail and sent Sandy and Malone to the hospital. "We're gonna need you both, so get fixed up."

Beltram got Kerrigan locked up in a cell next to Pasternak. "That should be good for listening," he laughed. He sent for the undertaker to take the bodies of Peters, Connor, and Ciarra. "No more Warm Springs," he said. "What a pleasure that'll be."

"Looks like it would make a fine resort," Endicott said. "Did Pasternak really own the place or just take it over."

"I don't know if there is a deed on that property or not," Beltram said. "The hot springs have been used for hundreds of years. The Paiute and Washoe Indians stopped often. Before Pasternak took the place over, pools had been built for the hot water."

"Put up some nice buildings and it would make a fine resort," Endicott said.

"You sound like a man with a plan, Butch," Calhoun said.

"The rock there is really good for building, there is fine hot mineral water bubbling out of the ground and would make a fine health spa. I've seen them in other places. I'll be at the courthouse when it opens in the morning."

Butch Endicott had had this conversation before, with Abe Curry, when they discussed where the rocks would be quarried for the mint building. The Warm Springs quarry was Endicott's choice and Curry agreed, but the hot springs was always in the back of the stone mason's mind. His conversations with the father of Carson City always included the idea of a real resort at the area.

"Mr. Curry said I shouldn't build everything all at once. It would be too expensive. I'll let the place pay for itself as we go. Good restaurant, small clinic, and those from the east can come west to be cured of what ails them," he laughed.

It was coming light, snow was falling in great waves, when Calhoun finally walked through the doors of his hotel. Morrison was in the café having breakfast. "Did you shoot the fool?" he asked.

"Nope. Gonna let his own people do it, back in Washington. Heard you burned down the Warm Springs Resort. Get the bad guys?"

"Brought one back alive. The others, not so much so. Got a little hot for a short time, but Pasternak's gang is out of business. Both Squash and Sandy got hit but they're okay. They're at the doc's now."

"Major wants us back right away. Get some sleep and we'll catch the evening train out."

CHAPTER 31

"Just about got her wrapped up, Slim. How's your arm coming?" Bull Morrison and his deputy were having breakfast in the St. Charles Hotel dining room. They weren't able to get out of town the day before because of legal matters. The district judge insisted the marshals testify at Pasternak's hearing.

"Butt still hurts, arm hurts, and I'm still one tired puppy, Bull. Glad this one's over. How the hell did Ivory live through his wounds we'll never know. He and Bricky will hang for sure, Pasternak will be alongside them."

Acting Sheriff Beltram and his chief deputy Sandy Ferris came in and joined them. "Got us a full jail, Marshal, thanks to you. Stopping that mint shipment robbery was your job but cleaning up corruption in Nevada's capital was the best thing you could do. The election is next month and the word around town this morning is sounding good for me."

"I'm glad to hear that, Tiny. You've got some fine help there, too. How's that hand feeling, Sandy?"

"Hurts like hell," Ferris laughed. "Doc says I'll still have full use, though. Broke half the bones and tore up tendons everywhere. Got some good news, too. Buffalo Butch Endicott and Abe Curry went into partnership and bought the Warm

Springs property. That man has big plans."

"Gonna have to change his name, though," Slim said. "Instead of Buffalo Butch, he's gonna have to call himself Doc Endicott. Half of us are alive because of him."

"Where's Squash? He should be here." Bull Morrison looked around for his other deputy. "That leg of his giving him trouble? Didn't look good in court yesterday."

"He was at the telegraph office when I walked over," Sandy Ferris said. "Said he'd catch up shortly."

"He's got serious wounds that needed special care, is what he told me." Slim Calhoun had a sly grin saying that. "There's a little farm girl named Gladys Wooster, out in Gold Creek Canyon, who he believes is the best nurse in the world. It is possible, Bull, that the marshal service may have seen the last of our Oglala warrior."

"My God in heaven," is all Bull Morrison could say.

Squash Malone limped up to the table and found a chair. "Well, Bull Morrison, I've made a big decision." He reached inside his buckskin vest and pulled his marshal's badge out. He almost fondled it for a minute before setting it on the table in front of Morrison. "Gonna give it up. My mother and father have a section of land in the Dakotas and are going to stake claim for me on adjoining land. I'm gonna marry that little Wooster girl and raise big cattle."

"That's hard work, Squash," Morrison said. "You up to it?"

"Can't be as hard as what you've had me doing these past few days. Damn, Bull, I've got holes in my body and muscles that ache. Gladys and I are gonna get married in Dayton and we're gonna ride north, have a flock of kids and a herd of cattle. You and Slim can come visit any time you want. There are always extra chores that will need to be taken care of."

"Of all the deputies I've ridden with, you are not the one

I would expect to quit the service." Bull Morrison picked up the worn, even slightly bent badge, and held it tight. I'm not gonna take it, Squash. There's always trouble in that country up there. I'll let the senior marshal up there know you might be available for special work. I won't let you quit."

He handed the badge back to the big man, got up and walked away from the table before Malone could say anything. Squash took the badge, held it tight for a long time before tucking it back in his pocket. "I'm kinda glad he did that," he murmured. Those left at the table were quiet as Squash Malone stood up, smiled at each one, and walked out the door.

A LOOK AT: NAME'S CORCORAN
TERRENCE CORCORAN
(TERRENCE CORCORAN WESTERN)

Terrence Corcoran carried a badge in Virginia City, Nevada until one day, in a drunken stupor, he shot the sheriff. Now he's returning to the Comstock looking to get his badge back and stumbles into a conspiracy that might put the sheriff, district attorney, and others in jail for a long time. A lovely working girl is brutally murdered, a Hungarian duke wants a Wells Fargo gold shipment, and the sheriff rehires him after first kicking him in a most tender spot. Corcoran was born on the ship bringing his family to this country, ran away to the frontier at an early age and brings his ideas of the old country and knowledge learned of the west to whatever mess he finds himself in. He's carried a badge, found himself in jail, and stands four-square for right, honor, and truth. You gotta love the guy.

AVAILABLE NOW

ABOUT THE AUTHOR

Reno, Nevada novelist, Johnny Gunn, is retired from a long career in journalism. He has worked in print, broadcast, and Internet, including a stint as publisher and editor of the Virginia City Legend. These days, Gunn spends most of his time writing novel length fiction, concentrating on the western genre. Or, you can find him down by the Truckee River with a fly rod in hand.

Gunn and his wife, Patty, live on a small hobby farm about twenty miles north of Reno, sharing space with a couple of horses, some meat rabbits, a flock of chickens, and one crazy goat.